A Candlelight Ecstasy Romance®

"I KNOW WE'RE VIRTUALLY STRANGERS, BUT WE WERE . . . LOVERS ONCE."

His voice sent a slow reminiscent ripple through her. "I know you must have thought I'd forgotten you, and I'll admit that I didn't recognize you when you walked into the courtroom, but it has been a long time, and you've changed."

His gaze drifted past her shoulder. "The day I met you was special, but at this moment I wish that day had never happened. I wish we were strangers, beginning a vacation romance."

She wanted to turn away from him, to feel indifferent toward this man who was a stranger to her. Yet she remembered the long-ago feel of him in her arms and knew he had never truly been a stranger at all.

CANDLELIGHT ECSTASY ROMANCES®

A DISTANT SUMMER

Karen Whittenburg

A CANDLELIGHT ECSTASY ROMANCE®

Published by
Dell Publishing Co., Inc.
1 Dag Hammarskjold Plaza
New York, New York 10017

Dell ® TM 681510, Dell Publishing Co., Inc.
Candlelight Ecstasy Romance®, 1,203,540, is a registered
trademark of Dell Publishing Co., Inc., New York, New York.

ISBN: 0-440-12049-7

Printed in the United States of America
First printing—April 1985

For David,
with many thanks

To Our Readers:

We have been delighted with your enthusiastic response to Candlelight Ecstasy Romances®, and we thank you for the interest you have shown in this exciting series.

In the upcoming months we will continue to present the distinctive sensuous love stories you have come to expect only from Ecstasy. We look forward to bringing you many more books from your favorite authors and also the very finest work from new authors of contemporary romantic fiction.

As always, we are striving to present the unique, absorbing love stories that you enjoy most—books that are more than ordinary romance. Your suggestions and comments are always welcome. Please write to us at the address below.

Sincerely,

The Editors
Candlelight Romances
1 Dag Hammarskjold Plaza
New York, New York 10017

CHAPTER ONE

She reminded him of someone . . . or perhaps of a distant summer.

The patina of dark wood haloed the champagne paleness of her hair. Subtly darkened brows arched over eyes that he knew would be blue, had to be blue to conform with her Nordic fairness. Delicate bone structure, creamy skin, small straight nose, lips tinted with moisture, she possessed all the fine points of arresting loveliness, and he watched her with a purely masculine approval.

He would have liked to touch her hair, to loosen the confining style, to feel the texture of its blond coolness in his hand. But even across the width of the courtroom he recognized the protective distance she unconsciously projected. She wore solitude as quietly as her clothing whispered good taste.

She stood just inside the heavy doors of the courtroom, alert to the tension in the air yet looking as if she had wandered through the wrong doorway. Scanning faces, her gaze searched past the crowd of observers to settle on him.

Tucker felt the impact of that single look lodge in his chest, and he immediately broke the unsolicited eye contact. He turned toward Mark Braison, the man beside him, and envied the calm, nerveless confidence the attorney affected. But Tucker found his gaze returning to the blonde, and he wondered how in hell he could even think of a woman, any woman, no matter how attractive, at the moment. She was still there, still watching him, and for a split second he thought she was smiling.

She wasn't smiling, though, and he didn't know why he'd had that sudden glimpse of her lips curving upward with seductive pleasure. Nerves. God, he was nervous. So much so that he was imagining things. Maybe he'd even imagined her. But as he narrowed his eyes in concentration, he decided she *was* real. Delicately, distractingly real.

Pushing away from the wooden doors, she walked to an unoccupied long bench and sat down. "Graceful," he added to his list of her feminine attributes. Then he forced himself to face front. But he was conscious of her continued observation, aware of her interest, and the knot of frustration in his chest tightened.

Why the presence of one more spectator among so many should bother him, he didn't understand, but he recognized the discomfort she caused. He wished the woman, whoever she might be, weren't here to witness the impending drama. Hell, he wished he weren't here either. He shouldn't be here, sitting at the defendant's table, prepared to defend his professional integrity against an unjust accusation.

It was all wrong. Mark was certain that there was no evidence to support a malpractice charge, no substance to the false claims that Tucker had violated his Hippocratic oath. Damn! He'd saved a life, and now, against every moral instinct, he was expected to justify that. This was the first day of jury selection, and Mark assured him it wouldn't go any further; but then no one had thought the litigation could progress to this point either.

It was a circus, Tucker thought, a caricature of both the medical and the legal professions. And the illusion of wrong had been carefully drawn by the skilled hands of an opportunist. If he turned around, Tucker knew he would see the pompous serenity of John Abernathy, an unappealing sight in the best of circumstances. Here in the solemn courtroom, it was a nauseating incongruity. Tucker knew, also without looking, that Sarah Abernathy was not present. She was safely tucked away in some sanitarium, where her testimony couldn't hinder the publicity-hungry ambitions of her husband.

Tucker shifted in his chair and glanced toward the back of the room again, toward the blonde. Dark lashes lowered, then lifted to capture him in the faint knowledge that she had been staring. Another, stronger sense of familiarity tugged at his remembrance. There was something, an indefinable memory, a certain feeling that he should know—

"All rise." The bailiff's voice brought instant at-

13

tention, and Kristina DuMont flowed to her feet with the rest of the courtroom crowd. The judge seated himself in a swirl of black robes, and in a moment Kris sank onto the wooden bench again. She shouldn't have come. She'd realized that the moment she saw him. Her heart jerked unsteadily with the thought.

Tucker McCain. Dr. McCain. She corrected herself as her gaze centered on the austerity of his navy jacket. The material pulled tautly across his back, and she tried to remember if his shoulders had seemed so broad then. He had been twenty-four . . . twenty-five? God, she didn't even know how old he'd been. She had been seventeen, barely, a very young, very childish seventeen.

Maturity suited him, she decided. Self-confidence lined the set of his shoulders; experience softened the stubborn angle of his chin. Gray feathered his dark hair; shadows deepened the intriguing shape of his eyes. He was much the same as the young man she'd known briefly, yet he was very different. Kris wondered if she would have recognized him under other circumstances. If she hadn't come to the courtroom expressly to see him, if she'd passed him by chance on the street, would she have known who he was?

Impossible to answer and a moot point besides. Curiosity had brought her here, to this room, to see Tucker McCain, and she had known him at once. She wondered about courtroom protocol. Could she just slip away now that she'd seen him? But both the attorneys stood and approached the judge's bench. Tucker glanced in her direction, and Kris responded with a questioning lift of her brow.

He smiled, turned away, then looked back as if he weren't sure he should. Did he recognize her? God, she hadn't considered that. She hadn't really considered anything except the persistent impulse to see him again, to discover if he'd changed.

It had been strictly chance that she'd even seen his name in the morning newspaper. Ordinarily on vacations she made little effort to keep up with current events. But this morning the *Rocky Mountain News* had come with coffee, compliments of the Brown Palace Hotel, and she had begun to read for the simple pleasure of knowing that she could do so at her leisure.

And then, there on the second page, his name had caught her unprepared, had whirled her back to another place, another time, another life.

The attorneys were returning to their chairs, and the judge began to speak. Kristina glanced toward the courtroom doors and sighed. She would stay for a few more minutes, then leave and continue her tour of Denver as planned. There was no reason this impulsive detour should change anything. She'd wanted to see him, and she had. It meant nothing.

Tucker heard the judge's announcement with mingled anger and relief: recessed until tomorrow morning. He leaned forward. "What in hell does this mean?"

Mark frowned and with a shrug lifted the file folder. "It means Abernathy got another delay and another day's worth of publicity. It means you and

I are going to walk out of here cool and collected, as if we had time to burn." Mark slipped the folder inside his briefcase and closed it with a frustrated click. "It means, my friend, that I'm going to spend the afternoon in my office waiting for a settlement offer."

Tucker drew in his breath. "After all this—"

"Abernathy's no fool. He knows he's milked this malpractice charge as long as he can without putting himself in jeopardy. I'm not fond of his attorney, but Walt Cooper is no one's fool either." Mark rose, and Tucker followed him to his feet. "No, Tucker, I think they're ready to call it quits."

"Damn! I'd like to shove that offer—"

"But you're not going to, remember? We've discussed this several times." With a touch of his hand to Tucker's shoulder, Mark adopted a smile and turned to leave. "Now, cool and collected."

"Sure thing." Tucker tightened his lips around the words. "I'll talk to you later." He walked beside his attorney to the doorway, then stopped to hold the heavy wooden door for a couple of people behind him. As they moved past him, he thought of the blonde and glanced back to the almost empty courtroom, but she wasn't there. A brief scrutiny of the anteroom proved equally futile, and he decided it was just as well. He didn't feel up to the polite social games necessary for initiating an acquaintance.

Tucker started to join the group waiting for an elevator but changed his mind and pulled open the door of the stairwell. It closed behind him with a quiet sound, and then he saw her. She was several steps below him on the landing, and her head was bent. The muted light above her tangled in the smoothness of her silvery hair, tinting it with an amber warmth. . . .

She looked up, and he knew. Memory shivered through him in indistinguishable images. Her eyes —not blue, as he'd supposed, but gray. Soft, mysterious gray. Now, suddenly, he remembered their color just as he remembered her hair tumbling over her bare shoulders, cloaked in the amber glow of fire. So long ago he'd all but forgotten. But seeing her, he wondered how he could have forgotten for even a moment.

He took a step forward and stopped. "Kristina?"

She froze, panic whispering through her veins. Too late to run, too late to consider the consequences of her impulse. Tucker McCain faced her, his voice rough with memory, a memory she'd hoped he couldn't possibly recall.

"Hello, Tucker," she said, answering the question in his dark eyes. "It's been a long time, hasn't it?"

He struggled for comprehension. "God, Kristina. I can't believe this. I didn't even know who— what are you doing here? Do you live in Denver? Are you—" There was so much to know, to discover, and he was suddenly awkward. "God, you're—you look wonderful. Lovelier even than I remembered."

Her smile bore little resemblance to the winsome smile he'd imagined earlier. She appeared in control, confident and comfortable with her femininity. He knew, on the other hand, he must look

17

as embarrassingly bewildered as he felt. His thoughts were a scramble of disjointed scenes as he tried to piece together his memories of this woman. He remembered her saying that she'd been twenty-one.

Self-assurance took hold with that bit of information. It all would come back to him if he didn't push it. Slowly he returned her smile. "I have this silly idea that I should say something very collegiate in honor of our first meeting, but all I can think of is the football team cheer. Not really appropriate for the courthouse." He paused, letting the hesitation mask his doubts. "We did meet at a football game, didn't we? God, it's been so long you've probably forgotten."

"No," she admitted with the complete awareness that he was struggling to remember even the most significant events of that day. "I mean, yes, it was a football game, at the University of Missouri. And no, I haven't forgotten. It was a . . . special day for me."

Best not to comment on that, he thought. But there were other things to know. "Have you had lunch? I know just the place to get reacquainted over a glass of wine and some of the best food in town."

"Oh, no, thank you," Kris answered too quickly. "I'm on vacation, and I've already made plans for this afternoon."

A shadow of disappointment altered the curve of his mouth. "I see. You're meeting someone. Your husband? Maybe the three of us—"

"No." Her interruption was automatic and

18

sounded brusque, even to her. She should have let him think she was married. But she couldn't. Perhaps because she'd lied to him before, it seemed imperative not to deceive him now. "I'm not meeting anyone."

"Then please have lunch with me." His blue eyes deepened to twilight, and she thought that the years had served only to enhance his charisma. She would have liked to accept, but it was impossible. Words of refusal formed, but he spoke first. "Don't refuse, Kristina. I'd really like to talk to you."

Talk? What could they talk about? She didn't know the etiquette for renewing an acquaintance with a man she'd spent one weekend with almost eleven years before. Still, she couldn't ignore the odd note in his voice. He needed to talk to someone, probably wanted to tell her about the court case. How ironic that Tucker McCain should need to talk to her. And how fitting that she found it so difficult to turn her back on him now.

What was the harm? It was only lunch. And maybe it would be good to give herself an opportunity to ask him a few of the questions that had always bothered her. Nothing specific, of course, but during the past years she'd learned how to elicit the information she wanted. It was, she soothed the voices of reason, just lunch. She would be careful about what she said. What could go wrong? "All right," she agreed. "Lunch."

When he walked down the stairs to her side, Kris knew she was taking an incredibly foolish risk. Everything could go wrong—so easily that her heart pounded with the possibility. Yet she smiled and accompanied him from the building, answering polite questions with polite answers, giving information, but revealing nothing of importance. *Yes, she was on vacation. No, she'd never been to Denver before. Yes, she liked the city very much. No, she was staying only until the end of the week.*

She didn't like the feeling of awkwardness that settled between them in the back seat of the taxi. She didn't like the awareness of Tucker, sitting so close that she was warmed with remembrance. But when he smiled, almost shyly, as if he also felt awkward with his thoughts, Kris knew memory wasn't the only cause of her disquiet.

It was the man beside her. It was the subtle physical strength of him, the long, sinewy length of his legs, the muscular hardness of arm that brushed against her shoulder with the motion of the cab. Her senses were alert to his every movement; her gaze was tempted again and again to his navy trouser-clad thighs.

He was tense, but she didn't actually believe she was responsible. His tension was a result of frustrations with the law and probably with the medical profession as well. She knew that without knowing quite how she knew. And it bothered her: not just the knowing but the sympathy that unsolicitedly winged from her heart to his.

"Are you staying in town long?" he asked, and then grimaced in apology. "I already asked that, didn't I?"

"Yes." She bathed her expression in pleasant understanding. "And I'm still staying only until the end of the week."

"Are you visiting friends in the area?"

"No. Denver just seemed like an interesting destination when I started driving. It's been a very beautiful trip. The Colorado scenery is indescribable."

"You drove all that way?" He paused and gave a short laugh. "I don't even know where you live. You might have driven over from Boulder."

"I might have, but it was a little out of the way, considering that Arkansas is southeast of here."

"Arkansas?" A minuscule frown creased his forehead. "But I thought—" Another self-directed laugh rumbled in his throat. "You've moved from Missouri, of course."

She smiled in wry concurrence. " 'Et tu, Brute'?"

"Yes, I also," he said with a glint of humor. "I could hardly wait to leave my home state behind. The fact that I was accepted at the medical college here helped stir my wanderlust. What about you?"

"I've never been much of a wanderer, except for vacations. The rest of the time I stay close to home."

"And family?"

An old pang tightened across her stomach. "No family, just home and friends."

His gaze brushed her cheek with a more intimate question, but he didn't ask. "Where are you staying in Denver?"

"The Brown Palace. Is there any other place?"

21

"Several, but none quite so steeped in tradition."

She smiled. He smiled. Silence clustered thickly in the narrow confines of the cab. She shouldn't have come. Kris accepted her judgment as she adjusted her position on the seat beside him and smoothed the crisp fabric of her skirt. There was no graceful way to excuse herself now. Why had she decided to vacation in Denver? And in all the vacations of the past why hadn't she ever, once, met a man who was as attractive, as physically compelling, as Tucker McCain? But she knew. She'd never met anyone else who could compare because she'd met Tucker first.

The taxi pulled to the curb, and in a matter of minutes she was walking under a green awning and into Café Giovanni. It was crowded but thinning in the lull between the lunch-hour and early-evening clientele. There was only a brief delay before she and Tucker were going up the curved stairway to the dining area.

Tucker seated himself across from her at a small out-of-the-way table, and Kris opened a menu and perused it without seeing at all.

"May I order for you?" The persuasive tone of his voice made her lower her menu, and she faced his dark sapphire eyes. And in that split second of contact she knew he could rearrange her life again if she wasn't careful.

"A cocktail?" he asked. "Or would you prefer wine?"

"Wine, I think. And something light to eat. A salad maybe?"

He nodded and spoke quietly to the waiter. Kris looked around the restaurant, noticed the exposed red brick walls, the plush forest-green carpet, but her attention was entirely on Tucker, on the easy confidence that seemed so much a part of him. She heard him order, and the wine he had chosen was Chablis. Against her will she wondered if he remembered the firelight diffused through crystal goblets or the wine she'd nervously spilled on the less than plush carpet. No, he barely recalled meeting her. Why would he remember the type of wine?

He shouldn't have ordered the Chablis, Tucker thought as he turned to watch Kristina's interested study of Café Giovanni. The moment the words had left his mouth, he'd realized the connection between that kind of wine and his first encounter with the woman now seated across from him. God, what a situation.

She was very lovely, and the intangible distance that shielded her intrigued him. Why hadn't he met her for the first time today? But since fate hadn't allowed that, why hadn't she taken her vacation in another month, a month in which his life wouldn't have been in upheaval, a month in which he could have given her his concentrated attention?

The thoughts evolved into a slow question, and he ran a pensive fingertip over the hemmed edge of his napkin. "Kristina? Why were you—How did you happen to be at the courthouse today?"

Her gaze returned to him with a hint of smoky apprehension. She glanced down as if weighing her response and then met his eyes. "I saw your name in the morning paper and I decided to go. I didn't intend to talk to you. I just was . . ."

Her voice trailed into an unsettling hush, and Tucker felt a spiral of disappointment. Curiosity had brought her into that courtroom. She had wanted to see *Dr.* McCain on the legal hot seat. Nothing more. Certainly not Tucker McCain, victim of circumstantial publicity, a man in need of a friend. He couldn't prevent himself from leaning back against his chair . . . away from her.

Kris recognized the defensive movement and knew that somehow she'd offended him. Even knowing she should not say more, she couldn't seem to prevent herself. "When I read the article about your—about the litigation, I couldn't believe it. I know how much, I mean, I remember that you told me, how much becoming a doctor meant to you. This lawsuit must be a nightmare."

"It hasn't been pleasant," he answered in cautious acknowledgment. "But then I don't suppose many malpractice suits are."

He had stressed the word, and Kris felt another tug at her sympathy. Malpractice. He must hate the very idea, and to have it associated with his career! Small wonder that he exuded such intensity. "Will the case be resolved soon? Out of court?"

"My attorney seems to think so, but . . ." He lifted his shoulders in a heavy shrug. "Frankly, I'm at the point where I don't give a damn whether or not it's ever resolved."

Oh, he gave a damn all right. Even a casual

observer could see just how much he cared—or how much he hurt. Why hadn't she simply skipped the newspaper that morning and gone ahead with her original plans? Then she wouldn't be here now, caring because he cared, hurting because he hurt. "You worked very hard to become a doctor, a *good* doctor."

He tilted his head slightly at her confident tone. "Did I tell you that, too?"

"There are things I don't have to be told."

The corners of his mouth curved upward but didn't quite become a smile. "Thank you, Kristina. It's comforting to know I have a champion in the state of Arkansas."

"You must have dozens, hundreds, of supporters here in Denver."

His only answer was to glance, as if impatient, in the direction the waiter had taken. Restless fingers danced along his napkin before curling into a fleeting fist, and then he brought his gaze to her. "Tell me about Arkansas."

Kris accepted his change of subject gracefully. "The capital is Little Rock. The population is somewhere around—"

He interrupted her. "I meant to say, tell me about *you.*"

She'd been hoping he wouldn't ask; she'd been wondering what she would say when he did. The napkin in her lap began to acquire nervous pleats. "I'm a newspaper editor. It's not a large publication, strictly small-town news, but I'm very proud of it."

His dark brows lifted in acknowledgment, and

Kris realized her defensiveness. She hated the un-expected feeling. After her first year at the *Maple Ridge Gazette* the guilty feeling that she should apologize for her career choice had vanished. Why should the old attitude reappear now? And why had she been so quick to classify herself by her work, as if the sum of her existence could be found in the equation of newsprint and ink?

"And where is this small town?"

"Arkansas." Her tone was flippant, but it was threaded with a quiet panic. He smiled, and Kris saw an unavoidable and perfectly legitimate ques-tion rising in his eyes. As it parted his lips, the waiter arrived with the wine, and she thought it couldn't have come at a better time. She didn't want to tell Tucker anything more about her life. Maybe he wouldn't ask.

"You've never married." Tucker offered the statement in the same careful way he extended a glass of wine, and just like that, he altered the mood and swept her into an ambiance of conflict-ing emotion.

Accepting the glass, she pretended an interest in the transparency of the drink. "Why do you say that?"

"Just a hunch." He took a slow sip of wine and set the glass on the table. For a long moment he stared at it. He didn't look at her, and she didn't look at him, at least not directly. But the longing to do so was enclosing her, tightening across her lungs, increasing the beat of her heart. It was hard to breathe, and she knew release would come sim-ply by lifting her eyes to his. But she must not.

"I'm not married," he said in an offhand manner. "There's never been time. Or maybe there's just never been a good reason. I don't know." His pause was contemplative; his soft sigh, weary. "That doesn't surprise you, does it?"

"No." She wasn't surprised at the information—she knew he would be the type of doctor whose commitment to medicine superseded any other commitment—but she was surprised that he'd mentioned the subject at all. The fact that he had was a measure of his uncertainty at the moment. It provided a glimpse of the vulnerable man beneath his cloak of confidence.

Silence came again, but this time she welcomed its comfort, and she sensed that Tucker did, too. Kristina continued to stare at her wineglass, remembering, oddly, that the last time—the *one* time—she'd been with this man, they had allowed not a second of silence. There had been a constant flow of words . . . looks . . . touches.

Luncheon arrived, and she banished memory to the safe past. Suddenly she was hungry and eager to lighten the mood and the pensive line of Tucker's smile. "Do you have a private practice in surgery?" She picked up a fork and poised it above her salad.

"Yes." Tucker focused first on the fork and then slowly raised his gaze to her face. Her gray eyes met his, and for an instant he thought her sudden cheerfulness faltered, but she recovered quickly with a general comment. And although he answered in the same vein, he did not recover as quickly. There had been something in that momentary exchange, something muted and almost fearful—but real. Very real.

Tucker tried to define that intangible reality during the course of the meal, but he never came close to solving the enigma. If there were shadows in her gray eyes, Kristina never allowed him another clear glimpse of them. She was quietly animated, talking around many topics of conversation yet drawing out his opinions and his attitudes with skilled subtlety.

He realized what she was doing without being truly aware of how she did it. He knew only that he was talking, voicing thoughts that seemed to form without conscious effort. What he said seemed unimportant. It was the type of conversation he might have had with any new acquaintance, but he had an odd sensation that she was learning more about him than he would have willingly told anyone else.

Each time he tried to turn the tables, to discover the person behind her beautifully delicate face, she gave answers that left him dissatisfied and hungry to know much more than she revealed. By the time he paid the check Tucker was certain that he wanted to see Kristina again.

"Have dinner with me tonight," he said, impulsively reaching across the table to touch her hand. Her fingers were cold, and he thought they trembled slightly beneath his. "We can make it late, if you prefer, and light."

She met his gaze and slowly withdrew her hand to her lap. "No. Thank you, Tucker . . . but no."

His palm lingered against the crispness of the

28

tablecloth as he sought again to penetrate the elusive veil of reserve that sheltered her. "Tomorrow, then. I'll phone your hotel room."

"I might not be there."

"I'll leave a message."

"That isn't necessary. Really. I appreciate your—"

"It *is* necessary, Kristina. I want to see you again. I *intend* to see you again." He couldn't understand her reluctance, couldn't explain his own persistence, but he knew he had never meant anything more sincerely.

She looked as if she might make another protest, but then a polite smile erased the impression. "I think I should be getting back to the hotel now. Thank you for lunch. It was very nice."

He rose just in time to grasp the back of her chair as she stood and tucked her purse under her arm. His hand went automatically to her waist, and, although she permitted the faint brush of his fingertips, he felt her become instantaneously alert. As they left the dining room and descended the stairs, nothing else was said, no smiles were exchanged. There were no glances that held a small treasure of meanings, and Tucker was lost in the puzzle.

When he followed her into the afternoon brightness, she turned to him. "Again, thank you. It was good to see you, Tucker."

A knot of frustration pulled taut inside him. She was going to walk out of his life as inexplicably as she'd walked in. He couldn't allow that, but what could he do to stop her? Without actually consider-

29

ing a course of action, he bent his head and whispered a zephyr-soft kiss to her lips. It was a mere touch, yet it told him more than he had learned during the entire afternoon.

There was a bond between his heart and hers. He didn't know if it had been forged in a long-forgotten moment or if it had bloomed into being within the past hour, but he didn't doubt its existence, and he didn't doubt that Kristina was aware of it, too.

"I'll phone you."

The husky tone of his voice sent a sweet unrest rippling through her composure. Kristina didn't protest. She simply turned from the dusky determination in his eyes and stepped inside a waiting taxi. Tucker came forward to close the door, leaning down to offer one last promise. "Tomorrow."

The cab pulled from the curb into the flow of traffic, and Kris knew that Tucker watched until her taxi rounded the corner. Only then did she let her head drop back against the cushioned seat. Only then did she rub the tension from her forehead. Only then did her shoulders slump and the quiet panic swirl helplessly inside her.

She had broken the cardinal rule, the one absolute in her life: "Don't look back." Today, for reasons she didn't completely understand, she had. And the consequences stretched before her like a deserted highway on a misty night. She couldn't see him again; she couldn't *not* see him again.

A trembling finger relived the brief caress of his kiss. Tomorrow. He would call tomorrow.

What was she going to do?

CHAPTER TWO

There were no messages waiting for Kris when she returned to the hotel the next afternoon. She had left early and spent the day out. By three o'clock she had walked past the courthouse twice, fighting a private battle of her own. At last, she'd decided not to complicate one mistake by making another. If Tucker phoned, she'd tell him she wasn't interested in furthering their acquaintance.

But Tucker hadn't phoned. The room clerk checked and said there were no messages. Standing at the front desk, Kris breathed a sigh of relief. But as she stepped inside the elevator, she admitted a definite splinter of disappointment.

She loosened the tension of her braided chignon with a restless fingertip and glanced around the confining cubicle. She was alone. The thought slipped through her mind; the feeling settled inside her. She was often alone. By choice, for the most part, but still alone. Perhaps it was a deeply ingrained defense left over from a childhood smothered in abundance but deficient in meaning.

The elevator doors opened, and she was determined to leave her sudden attack of self-pity behind. What was wrong with her today? There had been no messages, her heart answered. Maybe it was time to think about going home.

Home. Even in silence it sounded good, soothing and geared to forgetfulness. She had sometimes thought she would have drowned in the impersonal atmosphere of the world outside the Maple Ridge city limits. She had gone there in search of a hiding place and found a home and friends and, in many ways, a family.

Kris inserted her key and opened the door of her hotel room. It looked nice, neat, but it offered only a token welcome. What was she doing in a lonely hotel room in Denver, Colorado? Her friend Ruth insisted a yearly vacation was necessary for sanity, and usually Kris returned from a trip in total agreement. But not this time.

After tossing her purse on the bed, she slipped off her shoes and curled wearily into a chair. If she canceled her plans and went home a couple of days early, was there any possibility of avoiding Ruth's probing questions? No. Kris knew her tongue would run like a river the moment she heard Ruth's perceptive "You met someone, didn't you?"

She hadn't met "someone," though. She'd met Tucker, and that was the reason for her longing to run home, to seek a hiding place. Kris sighed and reached for the entertainment guide on the dressing table.

When the knock came, her heart jumped in startled surprise and the booklet slid from her hands to the floor. Who could—Tucker. No. But it might be—No. Disordered thoughts scrambled for recognition; a confusion of emotions accompanied her to the door. She touched the lock. Paused. The knock came again.

"Who is it?"

"Tucker."

Her fingers trembled. The lock was stubborn; her powers of reason were even more so. Finally, she opened the door to the dark-haired, blue-eyed reality of her past and faced again the private war of wanting things she couldn't hope to have.

Tucker was unprepared for the uncertainty he saw in her expression. Wispy strands of silvery gold feathered her face and neck. Her brightly patterned skirt looked somewhat crumpled; her blouse was unbuttoned to the shadowy cleft of her breast, as if she'd absently loosened it to a more comfortable level. Her feet were bare, her legs a creamy tan. He noticed the details of her appearance in that first moment, but her questioning gaze allowed him to do no more than notice.

The shadows were there, yet he thought there was a shy gladness, a definite welcome in the soft gray eyes. The mystery of her intrigued him, her casually disheveled beauty captured him, and all he could do was smile. "Hello," he said. "It's tomorrow."

"Yes."

Why did he feel so awkward with her? "May I come in?" he asked. She hesitated, and he held his breath. He'd had a suspicion she would ignore his messages, so he'd come in person and waited in the lobby for her to return. When finally he'd seen her at the front desk, an unexpected attack of nerves had kept him in his seat until she'd entered the elevator and disappeared from view. He'd followed slowly, knowing he wanted to see her but unsure if she would want to see him. And now it seemed as if she might close the door in his face. . . .

"Please, come in, Tucker." She stepped back, and he walked into the hotel room, not overly encouraged by her polite tone.

As she closed the door and moved toward the window, an aura of intimacy drifted into the air he breathed. He had never before been so aware of the fragility of a moment or of the many different levels of communication possible in a movement, a look, a silence. It was suddenly vital that he convince her to spend the evening with him.

"What happened today?" Kris turned her back to the curtained window and offered a tentative smile to conceal her disquiet. "At the courthouse."

"The insurance company settled with Abernathy yesterday afternoon."

"What? Just like that? But what about the trial?"

The rueful shrug of broad shoulders beneath a somber frown expressed a tightly controlled frustration. "Jury selection was just beginning. The trial hadn't actually begun, but my attorney thought it would be best to settle and avoid accruing any further expense."

"But the legal fees would have been taken care of in a judgment, wouldn't they? And you would have won the case. I'm sure of it."

A touch of gratitude lightened the sapphire of his eyes. "The insurance company isn't blessed with your foresight or your faith, Kristina. It wanted to play it safe. So as of this morning, the suit's been dropped, and for all practical purposes it's over."

"You don't sound as if you believe that."

His brows formed an arch of disillusionment. "Just because something has ended doesn't necessarily mean it's over."

Kris dropped her gaze, feeling the truth of his words in a dozen memories. She knew firsthand that some things were never over. "Despite the fact that the whole thing seems grossly unfair to you, I'm glad it's settled. I know you must be relieved."

"I'll feel better about it if you'll agree to celebrate with me tonight."

How could she refuse? Kris licked dry lips. "I'd love to, Tucker, but I can't. You see, I planned to—to—" *What?* She couldn't think beyond the moment and the tension clenching along his jawline.

"What is it, Kristina? Is it the lawsuit? Does it bother you that I was accused of malpractice? Is that the reason you're so reluctant?" His voice was edged with impatience as he shoved a hand into a trouser pocket in frustration. For a heart-hammering instant he held her gaze, and then control straightened his shoulders. "I'm sorry. That wasn't fair. It's just that I want very much to share this evening with you."

Her breath hung precariously at the base of her throat, and the thought that this wasn't really hap-

35

pening spiraled aimlessly inside her. Oh, God. She'd never dreamed she would see him again. She'd thought it was over long, long ago. If she'd had any idea of the sheer physical attraction that would scintillate between them . . . If she'd even suspected the emotional pull his unspoken needs could evoke . . .

Even had she realized the danger, Kris admitted, it wouldn't have changed this moment of self-knowledge. Elemental longings drew her to Tucker now, just as they had drawn her to him years before. She'd been naïve, innocent, then. But she'd been only slightly less so in thinking she could see him again without igniting embers that should long since have grown cold. And now she was helpless before the tiny flicker of warmth inside her.

She pressed her lips together before drawing a low breath of courage. "Tucker, I'm very flattered by your interest, but the truth is . . ." And there the impending lie faltered with the cautiously self-protective angle of his chin.

When she didn't continue, the corners of his mouth lifted in a rueful smile. "The truth is there's someone else, isn't there? Someone waiting for you in Arkansas."

"No." She denied it without understanding why she did so. Her hand went to her temple, brushed distractedly at the wispy blond strands that had strayed from the chignon. "And it has nothing to do with your lawsuit. If I were looking for a vacation romance, Tucker, I'd like to believe I might find it with you, but I'm not looking."

Seconds ticked past in leisurely succession, but his blue eyes didn't waver in their intense regard. "Somehow I don't think that matters, Kristina. Whether or not we were looking, we've found something. Something special. I can't explain how I know that or why I think you know it, too, but I can tell you that I have no intention of letting it end here."

Her logic stumbled into a solid wall as she tried to understand his persistence, tried to think of a believable refutation. She stroked the back of the chair beside her with restive fingers. "I'm not good at social games, Tucker."

"Then we'll skip the games and start the evening with a little honesty."

Her chin lifted; her gaze locked with his in a second of startled precognition. He was going to mention the past, *their past.* She could almost see the words forming on his lips and knew she had to stop him. She wasn't prepared for honesty. It was *her* secret, her mistake, her regret. He had no right to remember.

"Kristina?" he said in a hushed, throaty tone. "There's not a subtle way of bringing up this subject, but I think we should get it into the open."

For all her resolve, not a sound would come from her lips. She stood, watching him, aware of the betraying tension in the casual combing of his hand through his hair, aware of her own spiraling doubts. "Don't, Tucker, please." She had no idea if the words were whispered about the room or simply echoed in her mind.

"I know we're virtually strangers, but we were

. . . lovers once." His voice, husky with decision, was like the first sip of a summer wine, and it became a slow reminiscent ripple through her veins. "I know you must have thought I'd forgotten, and I'll admit that I didn't recognize you when you first walked into the courtroom yesterday; but it has been a long time, and you've changed." The wry tilt of his mouth was touchingly brief. "I know I've changed a little myself. But you seemed different, so reserved. Not like the winsome girl I remembered."

His gaze drifted past her shoulder and returned to touch her in confession. "The day I met you was special for me, too, Kristina, but at this moment I wish to God that day had never happened. I wish we were strangers, taking the first steps toward a vacation romance."

She wanted to turn her back to him. She wanted to close her eyes to the sincerity in his. She wanted to feel a healthy indifference toward this man who was in every way a stranger to her. Yet she remembered the long-ago feel of him in her arms and knew he had never truly been a stranger at all.

"It did happen, Tucker," she whispered softly, thinking that if she were honest, if she told the truth, he'd leave and she'd never see him again.

"Yes, but I can't see any reason to let that stand between us now. We were different people then. I know I looked at life through much narrower eyes in my premed days. There wasn't time for relationships, for anything except ambition."

He rubbed the back of his neck, and a frown creased one lean cheek. "We had one short weekend together. At the time that was all I could offer. Now I can only wish I'd had the foresight to realize just how special that one weekend was."

She had known. Kris focused sightlessly on a tiny flaw in the carpet and wondered how, in her adolescent frenzy to grow up, she had recognized emotions that were far beyond her experience. She had gone in search of a purely physical awakening and found tenderness, understanding, and a communion of thoughts and feelings. For one weekend, however fleeting, she had belonged with Tucker.

The muted sound of his footsteps reclaimed her attention, and she glanced up to meet his gaze, closer now and penetratingly clear. "I want to know you now, Kristina. I want to discover the woman you've become. Do you think we could start over? Forget we'd met before yesterday?"

Forget? What sweet ironies fate could play. Tucker had given her the perfect opening to tell him why she couldn't forget. And in the same instant he'd offered a temporary but tempting forgetfulness.

"I'm leaving at the end of the week, Tucker. That's only two days away." It was a weak argument, hardly worth her effort. Kristina could see the glimmer of relief ease across his expression; she could feel an old recklessness stirring inside her.

"If two days is all you can offer, then that's all I'll ask for." Tucker made himself smile to reassure her. She was still hesitant, still unsure of him, and he wanted her to be sure. He wondered what or who had hurt her to create such a convincing veneer of solitude. But it was just a veneer; he sensed that she was reaching out to him despite herself.

And oh, how he wanted to reach for her and hold her in his arms. Or was it that he wanted to be held by her? She was a part of something he'd lost a long time ago, something he felt he had to recapture. "Who knows?" he said casually, carefully. "You might decide Denver is worth a little extra time."

"I'm leaving on Saturday." Her voice was steady and definite.

"Then let's not waste a minute," he said, making his tone just as steady, just as definite as hers. "What would you like to do? A late lunch, an early dinner, the theater, a movie, a drive, a walk, cross-country skiing, a noisy crowd, or quiet conversation?"

Amusement dawned in her gray eyes, which watched him with compelling mystery. "Can we manage all that in one evening?"

"Only if we forget about the late lunch."

Her low laughter splashed a lazy tide of pleasure over him and made him dramatically aware of the privacy surrounding them. She was so near he could smell the fragile scent of her cologne, see the faint sheen of moisture on her lips, hear the sounds of her uneven breathing. His smile faded into a throat-tightening desire as his gaze sought the contours of her mouth.

"Why don't I meet you downstairs in an hour?" Kristina controlled the betraying tremor in her voice as she dispelled the moment of intimacy

40

with cool deliberation. "By that time you may have figured out a way to fit everything into one night."

He traced a lingering visual touch from the corner of her lips to her forehead and left her skin feeling flushed and warm. "Everything?" he asked with soft suggestion. "Well, I'll do my best, Kristina."

She matched his half-smile, fighting the warning rumble of good judgment all the way. When he turned and moved slowly to the door, Kris followed, keeping a cushion of intangible distance between them. He opened the door, and she braced her hand against the knob, waiting for something she couldn't name.

Their eyes met in the shadowy doorway: hers troubled and apprehensive, his comforting and reassuring. Like the company of an old friend on a winter night, memories wrapped about her thoughts, memories that reminded her of the hours she'd spent wondering about this man who faced her now, a virile, appealing answer to so many questions. Who would ever know, who would even care if she acted impulsively this one time?

"I'll be downstairs," she said quietly, "in an hour."

"I'll be waiting. Making plans and . . . just waiting."

Anticipation diffused through her. Somewhere down the hall a radio filtered the air with a dimmed melody. The muffled chime of an elevator bell signaled the comings and goings of a world that seemed curiously removed. But it didn't matter. For tonight, for the next two days, nothing mattered except Tucker McCain and Kristina DuMont, who had once been lovers but who were now not quite strangers.

"An hour." She began to close the door, but he stood steadfast in the doorway as if reluctant to leave even for a short time.

His smile came in an easy blend of diffident amusement, and Kris curled her toes against the carpet in helpless response. "I seem to be having a little trouble getting down to the lobby," he said.

A slow, sweet magic drifted across her nape and settled on her lips. "I seem to be having some trouble closing this door. At this rate we'll have to forget about dinner. Maybe the movie, too."

His hand lifted, and she felt a gentle tug at her temple as he curled a strand of hair around his fingertip. It was a familiarity that frightened her a little by the pleasurable sensation it evoked. She watched his eyes darken as he released the curl with lingering reluctance.

"I'll be downstairs," he repeated with a husky sigh, "waiting."

He took a step back, and she closed the door. A measure of sanity returned with the click of the latch, and Kris pressed her forehead against the barrier. Was she being impulsive? Or merely foolish?

Both, undoubtedly, yet she felt a restless excitement, a sense of freedom. Hadn't she always wished—in her most secret fantasies—that one day she would meet him again? And hadn't she always known that when she did, it would be magic?

For years she'd denied it, and she knew, with absolute certainty, that it was a mistake to admit it now. She pushed away from the door and walked to the middle of the suite. In smooth, graceful pirouette she surveyed the hotel room and wondered how it suddenly could seem so homelike and cozy.

Tucker was waiting. Kris sank to the edge of the bed and let her mind absorb that awesome reality. Tucker was waiting for her as if the yesterday of eleven years had never happened. *Forget,* he'd said.

A bittersweet knot closed her throat. She couldn't forget, but she could pretend—just until Saturday. It surely wasn't such a terrible thing to pretend for a few days? To steal a moment simply for the enjoyment it promised?

Once that had been her ultimate and only goal: to enjoy everything the world had to offer; to steal moments that rightfully belonged to tomorrow. She had been so young—so incredibly, arrogantly young—on the sunny afternoon the world had offered her Tucker McCain.

Kris pulled a pillow from beneath the colorful bedspread and held it in her arms, letting her fingers stroke the crisp white fabric in remembrance. How had she been able to lie so convincingly that Tucker had actually believed she was twenty-one? A college sophomore? A woman with real purpose in her life?

Purpose? She closed her eyes against the uncomfortable memories that word recalled. Her one purpose since age ten had been to grow up as quickly and with as much melodrama as she could manufacture. She had been rebellious and wild, ready to try anything regardless of consequences.

But Kristina Kathleen DuMont, youngest child, only daughter, and "little darling" of Patrick Wells DuMont, rarely even knew the consequences of her impetuous acts. Papa was always there to rescue her, to protect the family pride, and to warn her that someday she'd push him too far.

And she'd kept pushing, seeking attention in the only way she knew, wishing someone would listen to what she had to say, wanting desperately to feel needed, to belong.

Then, suddenly, there was Tucker, who treated her as if she were special, as if what she said mattered. And despite her lack of experience, she'd known that to him she *did* matter, if only for a little while. She'd discovered that it was possible to share thoughts and feelings. For a few wonderful hours her carefully constructed lies became truth, and she caught a glimpse of the person she wanted to be, of the future that could be hers.

The pillowcase crumpled into a dozen wrinkles beneath her hand, and Kris began absently to smooth them. Of all the college seniors on the University of Missouri campus that Saturday, why had she met the one man who could have been more, so much more, to her than a lover? After all, she'd planned to lose only her virginity, not her heart.

But falling in love with Tucker came as easily as

the lies she told him, and the hours spent in his arms were a beautiful fantasy that she was certain would last an eternity. He'd told her, openly and honestly, that he had neither time nor commitment for a long-term relationship, but at seventeen she'd been positive he didn't mean it.

Her perfect alibi had crashed about her the moment she'd returned home. The very real problem of angry, alienated parents had blurred the dreamlike wonder of her weekend with Tucker, but Kristina had accepted the threats, the lectures, and the dire warnings without excuse. She hoarded the memory of stolen moments as if it were the key to her diary, and she didn't tell anyone, didn't even dare breathe Tucker's name against her satin sheets.

It was two weeks before she risked mailing a letter to him, and she poured her heart's imaginings onto the pastel pages. Within a few days, she held his answer: *He'd thought she understood there was no future for them, no possibility of a lasting relationship. Maybe it would be best if they didn't see each other again.*

Even fanciful, resilient youth couldn't misinterpret his rejection, so Kristina told herself she didn't care. But when she realized she was pregnant, she knew she had to care—because no one else did.

Her second letter to Tucker was returned, unopened and unread. Her family closed ranks, chastening her with disapproving silence and waiting for her to come to terms with the idea of a quick no-nonsense abortion.

Even now, so many years later, Kris could feel the utter loneliness of those days in which she'd wrestled with the consequences of her careless immaturity. But in the end she'd made the only honest choice she could make: responsibility.

With a heavy sigh Kris tossed the pillow aside and rose to walk to the window. She didn't often think about that time in her life. Of course, it was impossible not to think of it now—now, when the father of her child was waiting downstairs for her.

Dear God! What right did she have to pretend she'd never met Tucker before when her body, her emotions, her very life, bore the imprint of his touch? She should have told him all those years ago. She should have written a third letter and a fourth. She should have told him yesterday. Or today.

But she wasn't going to tell him at all. Kris knew it as well as she knew that she was going downstairs to meet him in a matter of minutes. It wasn't within the boundaries of her willpower to confess now. She had made countless mistakes, and she had paid dearly. There had to be a limit to the sacrifices demanded by the past.

On Saturday she would leave Denver, and her life would continue on in its steady, contented routine. Tucker would return to his medical practice, and in a few weeks he'd forget about her—as he'd done before. What possible harm could come from a brief vacation romance?

Slowly her gaze turned to the stark white pillow contrasted with the bright spread. Tomorrow or the next day she would share that bed with

Tucker. She knew and accepted her inevitable desire with a confused sense of wonder. But was she really prepared for the possible consequences this time? Physically, yes. There would be no chance of another unplanned pregnancy. But in other ways was she prepared for the regrets she would undoubtedly harbor when Saturday arrived?

Kris moved to lift the pillow and nestle it back in place. She had no way of knowing the answer. She wasn't even sure she wanted to know. For now she was aware only that Tucker was waiting . . . and she felt wondrously, magically alive.

CHAPTER THREE

Tucker glanced at his watch, looked around the hotel lobby, and then glanced again at the face on his wrist. Almost time. Any second now he would see Kristina walking toward him. He wished she would hurry. He couldn't remember ever being so anxious to be with a woman. It was the air of mystery about her, he decided. That and the fact that she had known him before.

The reasoning brought frown lines to his forehead, and he wished for a drink to dull the analytical turn of his thoughts. Was he really intrigued by Kristina? Or was it more his own frustration with life in general that created this restless longing within him?

Hell! He didn't want to examine his motivation. He didn't care *why* he wanted to be with her. He knew only that he did. The next two days held a tantalizing promise, and he'd be damned if he'd spend them dissecting his every thought.

All right, she was a link—if only a very small one —to a simpler time in his life, a time when adding an M.D. to his name was the singular focus of his existence. If her appeal was rooted in his craving for that simpler time, well, she'd be gone in two days, and maybe a little of his frustrated confusion would vanish with her. If she was merely a pleasing combination of feminine charms, well, two days should be more than enough to sate his infatuation.

He'd never considered himself a completely self-sufficient man. His energetic, supportive family had reared him with a healthy appreciation for the importance of loving, give-and-take relationships, but all his close relatives were now miles and years removed from his everyday life. He had a large circle of acquaintances, a few really close friends, and he had his career. Over the years he'd had a couple of serious love interests. He'd even been engaged once, but when he'd realized how little it bothered him to leave her in the mornings, how much in fact he looked forward to getting to the hospital, he'd ended the relationship.

There had been no one special since, and he hadn't felt particularly dissatisfied. His life was a busy routine of interwoven schedules, and his medical practice provided enough challenge and purpose to carry him for years to come.

Or at least it had. Sudden anger filtered through him, and he began to drum his fingers on the arm of the chair. What an injustice that he, who had wanted, planned, scraped, and sacrificed to become a doctor, could see it all slipping from his grasp for no better reason than to feed the ambition of a man like Abernathy.

Damn! Tucker pulled his impotent rage into a tight fist. Abernathy would no doubt be governor one day, but there would be no reparation to the people he'd ruined in order to get there. Sarah Abernathy, for one. Tucker, for another.

He slowly relaxed his fist and then massaged the clenched muscles at his neck. If only he could blame the entire affair on someone else, but Tucker knew he'd made his share of mistakes. As soon as the lawsuit had been filed, he'd begun easing away from his practice, referring patients to another surgeon, making preparations to fight for his "rights." Colleagues advised him to ignore the loss of a small percentage of patients, friends urged him to put the charges from his mind and continue as if nothing had happened, but he couldn't. To be publicly, even when wrongfully, accused of misusing his hard-earned knowledge and skill had dealt a crippling blow to his belief in himself, as a doctor and as a man.

He couldn't explain it to anyone, didn't fully understand it himself, but he recognized a core of doubt in the one area of his life that he'd thought was invincible. He'd have to face it, have to make some decisions soon, but not yet. For now he wanted to forget everything and everyone except Kristina, who knew nothing about him but believed in him anyway.

His hand returned to tap impatiently against the chair arm, and then he saw her. Hesitating at the base of the hotel's famous staircase, she scanned the lobby, and then she moved toward the place where he sat waiting. She had exchanged the skirt and blouse for black slacks, a vividly striped top, and a bright jade-colored jacket. She looked sophisticated in a casual, unselfconscious way, but it was the shyly innocent tilt of her chin that created the hollow sensation in the pit of his stomach.

He stood without being truly aware of his action and barely restrained the hand that lifted automatically to straighten his tie. Two days weren't going to begin to be enough. "Kristina?"

In the pause after he had called her name, Kris let a delicious fantasy wrap about her. She was going out to dinner with a man she'd just met—a man whose good looks pleased her; a man whose innate masculinity excited her; a man whose smile cloaked her in velvet. She, Kristina DuMont, had no past before this moment, no future beyond the next few hours. The golden present was all that she had to consider.

"Hello, Tucker." Her voice drifted forward with the carefree effort of a cloud. "I'm sorry to have kept you waiting so long."

"It didn't seem long at all."

The throaty denial came as he walked forward to reach her. Kris felt a spiraling awareness open inside her. "Which way to the ski slopes?" she asked lightly. "And just as a matter of interest, do we pass any hot dog stands on the way?"

His smile was slow, easy, and very, very nice. "Trust me. I know a place where the hot dogs are truly worthy of their mustard. And the root beer is served in thick frosted mugs."

"How long will it take to get there?"

"Anywhere from twenty minutes to several hours, depending on whether we decide to walk or drive."

"I was hoping you'd suggest a drive. My feet already have an intimate acquaintance with the grass roots of Denver."

His gaze dropped to her feet, lingered on the bare strip of skin not covered by her black canvas slip-ons, and Kris had a sudden loss of breath. His dark hair was attractively disheveled; his expression, subtly sensual. His clothing was a well-tailored contrast of tans and navy blue, but his appeal lay in the determined self-confidence, the sense of purpose, that defined his features with gentle strength. He was vulnerable at the moment—she recognized that—but she didn't think anything could interfere with his life for long.

His eyes returned to hers with a ready mischief. "If you're having trouble with your feet, I can carry you to the car."

"You're too kind, Tucker, but I believe I can hobble as far as the street."

"I parked quite a distance from the door."

"I'll manage."

He fell into step beside her, amusement a subdued slant at the corners of his mouth. Although he didn't touch her, there was a feeling of closeness, an intangible communication as if he knew he *could* touch her but preferred to savor the knowledge rather than test its truth.

And in truth he didn't need to touch her. The mere fact of his nearness kept her heart pounding, kept her breath shallow. Kris couldn't help noticing the way his movements corresponded with hers, even down to his timing as he stepped ahead of her to open the door. She and Tucker were in tune, one with the other. But then, wasn't that just as it should be in a fantasy?

During the following hours, though, Kris found it increasingly difficult to remember that she was in the midst of a fantasy. Tucker was decidedly real, genuinely eager to talk to her about important and not so important issues of everyday living —like the advantages of using brown mustard in preference to yellow; like the vagarious nature of the weather; like the fundamental differences between listening to a talk show on the radio and watching one on television.

By the time they returned to the hotel, long after the moon was a silver shadow on the Denver skyline, Kristina felt completely comfortable with him. Or at least as comfortable as it was possible to be with her body on a natural high of awareness. Inevitably there had been moments throughout the evening when memory caught her unprotected, when she remembered things she didn't want to remember. But more often the moments had been composed of subtly enticing looks or light, exhilarating touches, casual in their inception but intimately serious as they lingered.

Tucker *was* special. There was no denying it, no wishing it were the simple imagining of her heart. If she *had* met him for the first time only yesterday, she would have been feeling the same sense of discovery, the same magic. Eleven years before, she had taken his tenderness and understanding for granted, not truly appreciating the special spark of attraction between them—a spark that she had searched for in other men since but had never found. Did Tucker feel it, too? Even after all this time?

Kristina knew she didn't need to ask. As she walked beside him down the hallway toward her room, his steps matched hers in procrastinating slowness. Their easy come-and-go conversation had lagged into a hesitant silence when they entered the hotel, and "good night" already hung heavily in the surrounding air.

Her numbered door came into view, and a thick indecision swelled in her throat. Should she invite him in? No, she couldn't. Not now, not until she was more sure of herself. Not until the question of invitation faded into the answer.

"Here we are." The husky inflection of his voice swept her thoughts to oblivion. The brush of his hand against her arm swirled through her like the warning rumble of a distant thunder.

She lifted her gaze to his and stared, unsmiling, into the cloudy twilight of his eyes. "Yes," she murmured. "Thank you, Tucker."

"For what?"

"For tonight." It was difficult for her to catch her breath, hard to speak over the faint echoing beat of her heart. "For the dinner. For the drive. For everything."

"My motives were entirely selfish, Kristina." A wry lift at one corner of his mouth gave the illusion of a smile. "I don't want you ever to forget this vacation . . . or me."

The knot in her throat grew even tighter, and she placed a palm against the wall behind her for support. "I won't forget."

He took a step nearer, his hand coming to rest on the doorjamb beside her, his expression softening with exquisite promise. "I'm not taking any chances. By Saturday there isn't going to be a single doubt, in my mind or in yours."

Kris moistened her lips, and her eyelids began to feel weighted with helpless expectation. "You're very sure of yourself, Tucker McCain."

"Yes. I guess I am." A thread of surprise wove his agreement into a caressing warmth that came close—very close—to her waiting lips. She looked down and away from his softly searching regard, wanting, yearning to taste the remembered texture of his kiss and afraid, so afraid to yield to the moment. She stared hard at the dark pattern of his tie until his thumb nestled a gentle pressure beneath her chin. Then slowly, carefully, at his insistence, she raised her face to his and relinquished her apprehension to the hands that now cupped her shoulders.

"Kristina."

Never had she heard a sound so low or so wondrously tender. Never had she needed a kiss so desperately or felt as if she were melting with the sheer knowledge that she was about to receive one. And with the first, tentative blending of lips she knew she would never forget these stolen seconds of enchantment. As his arms went around her, pulling her into his embrace, she moved willingly to savor the feel of his body against hers. A sensation of quiet pleasure rippled from her neck down her spine and ended in a faint tremor along her thighs. It was followed by a second and a third, and Kris found herself holding Tucker for the strength he represented.

An endless spool of responses wound upward from her toes, downward from the heated joining of her lips with his, and outward from her soul. In those timeless moments Kris knew the magnitude of her bonding to this man. It was past mistakes and a future that could never be. It was lies and truth, deception and honesty, all the things she should have told him and all the words she would never say. He held her by a slender thread, a once-in-a-lifetime emotion, that stretched from her wild and reckless youth to the restraints and responsibilities of her present. It wasn't going to end on Saturday. For now and always a part of her belonged with Tucker, and reclaiming it was beyond her ability . . . or her will.

The kiss deepened, became a languid desire, and ebbed to a reluctant retreat. When he drew back, then returned with a clinging, almost teasing series of caresses, Kris let her palms slide inside the nubbed fabric of his jacket. The silken lining against the backs of her hands felt warm; the pulsing heat beneath her fingertips was a heady rhythm that ached inside her. Tucker's sigh whispered first to her tactile senses before she felt its breath on her face and heard its echo in her heart.

She rested briefly in the sensual shelter of his arms before she looked up and lost her transient contentment to the tilt of his smile. A restless urgency tangled with years of carefully learned control. Kris pulled away and began a mindless rummaging through her purse for the room key.

Without a word Tucker ended her search, unlocked the door, and gallantly offered the key. The cool metal against her fingers brought her gaze to his once again, but she could read nothing beyond the midnight intensity in his eyes. "Good night, Kristina," he said, and bent to brush her mouth with tenderness one last time. Then he turned and walked away.

She watched him walk out of sight before she stepped inside her room and closed the door. With movements that trembled more than a little, she secured the lock and laid her purse on the dressing table. She started to place the key beside it but paused. With a contemplative fingertip, she traced the outline of the key and wondered if Tucker had thought about coming in with her. Reason told her that he had. Intuition told her that even if she'd asked, he would have refused.

It was unsettling, yet Kris was glad for the interlude. Tonight she would think about him, relive the past few hours, and fall asleep with the memory of his kiss. Whether he had sensed her doubts or simply offered her time to savor a sweet anticipation, Tucker had given her one more special moment to ensure that she would always remember. And as long as the fantasy lingered, she wouldn't even try to forget.

Morning came with the irritating jangle of the phone and the soothing tone of Tucker's voice. "Were you dreaming of me?"

Kristina stretched beneath the crisp sheets, feeling a wave of sleepy arousal drift through her awakening limbs. "If I were, would I tell you?"

"Wouldn't you?"

"No, I don't think I would." She cleared the night huskiness from her throat. "If nothing else, it might keep you from awakening me so early. This is my vacation, you know."

"And you're dreaming it away. I've been awake for hours."

"Hours?" she questioned, raising herself on an elbow and allowing the sheet to slide slowly to her waist as she squinted at the clock.

"Actually it's been only about twenty minutes, but it seems like hours."

At the hint of impatient humor in his words, her toes curled with an unexpected tingle of pleasure. "Why don't we make it hours and I'll go back to sleep?"

There was a pause, and then she heard the rough texture of his voice. "You're teasing . . . and so early, too." Another less certain pause followed. "You don't really want to—"

"No," she said softly, with a fleeting image of awakening in his arms. "How soon will you be here?"

"A half hour? Less? I'll come upstairs."

"That won't be enough time, Tucker."

His sigh was revealing. "All right, I'll wait in the dining room. I'll order coffee or something, but, Kris"—his tone deepened seductively—"don't keep me waiting too long. Please?"

Any further protest she might have made dwin-

58

dled to incoherence with his quiet persuasion. "I'll be there as soon as I can. And, Tucker?"

"Yes?"

"Good morning."

She could feel his smile singing through the telephone wires to reach her. "Good morning," he answered.

The morning progressed into afternoon at a lazy pace, and Kristina enjoyed the novelty of sharing a leisurely day with Tucker. She felt simultaneously relaxed and exhilarated. The anticipation of private moments together flavored their conversation with unspoken urgency, but the hours slipped past with no sense of haste.

Kris resolutely turned a deaf ear whenever conscience intruded into her thoughts. Logic had no part in her impulsive break from reality . . . until Saturday, when she would have to sweep the cobweb dreams from her heart.

Tucker made it easy to pretend that the world was theirs for the asking and that "tomorrow" was merely a synonym for "today." There was only one blemish on the golden glow of her day, and it occurred while she and Tucker window-shopped in Larimer Square.

"I thought real doctors always carried emergency beepers," she said teasingly.

His answer followed a sobering pause. "Not always."

"Come to think of it," she persisted with innocent cheerfulness, "I haven't seen you so much as glance at a telephone either last night or today. Are you off duty or out of practice or something?"

" 'Out of practice' about sums it up." The bitter inflection in his voice caught her unprepared, but in an instant he regained control. "Actually I'm just taking a breather from my medical practice right now. It feels pretty nice not to be on call, especially when I'm with you. This is one time I'd resent the intrusions."

Kris didn't doubt his sincerity, but she did wonder if perhaps he resented the *absence* of intrusions more. "Tell me what happened, Tucker," she asked quietly.

For a moment she thought he was going to ignore or deliberately misunderstand her request, but then slowly his defenses lowered, and as they walked past store after store in the shopping mall, the story of Sarah Abernathy unfolded.

Sarah had been referred to Tucker by another doctor, a trusted colleague. The facts had seemed straightforward and concise. He'd concurred with the diagnosis and agreed with both the other doctor and Sarah that a hysterectomy would solve her problems. The surgery was performed; the early stages of a malignancy were arrested. No complications. Case closed.

He'd been astounded when the lawsuit was filed, furious when it wasn't immediately dismissed, and frustrated as hell when he realized his inability to halt the widening ripple of consequences. John Abernathy alleged that he had suffered a loss of love, trust, and conjugal fellowship in his marriage because he had not been consulted *by the physician* before such a "radical" treatment as surgery was performed.

"Alienation of affection" and "consortium" were the legal terms bandied about most often. But the words that drew sympathy from the general public seemed to be those spoken ostensibly in private and then subsequently printed in the newspaper—words like "Sarah's emotional distress," "sanitarium," and "the children we will never have."

Tucker had yet to understand fully how he could be held responsible for the lack of communication between a husband and wife. In truth, he'd believed, been assured by the wife in question, that her husband both knew and approved the decision. There had been no way of knowing that John Abernathy was out of the country at the time or that he hadn't known about the operation because Sarah lived in constant fear of incurring her husband's displeasure.

Tucker felt sorry for the pathetic Sarah, who was a victim of her husband's wealth and relentless ambition and a prisoner of her own weakness. But that didn't change the malpractice charge or his appointment cancellations once news of the lawsuit had leaked to the media.

"But how could anyone sue *you* over something like that?" Kris protested when Tucker stopped speaking. "It's insane!"

"It's also the right of any American to sue anyone he damn well pleases—for any reason. Most nuisance cases are thrown out of court. I just happened to be sued by a man who knew exactly how

61

far he could stretch the integrity of our legal system."

"But why didn't the insurance company let it go to trial? Surely the weight of evidence was in your favor?"

"You can never be sure how a jury will decide, Kris. I wanted to fight, but after a while I realized that the damage to my career happened the moment the news went to press. And that sort of damage lingers no matter what the jury's verdict may be."

Kris frowned, conceding his point but still reluctant to believe. "But what about Sarah Abernathy? Wouldn't her testimony have proved your innocence?"

"She was safely out of state before the lawsuit was even filed. I'm not sure she would have done me any favors by testifying anyway. The woman has an unhealthy fear of her husband." He shook his head in derision. "Now that I have some personal experience with the man, I can understand how she feels. He's an incredibly smooth talker with the influence and money to back up anything he chooses to say."

"But surely the truth—"

Tucker shrugged. "The truth doesn't seem to be of much interest to anyone but me."

"It's so damned unfair!" she stated in sympathetic frustration.

"Yes" was his only response before the subject was dropped . . . forever, as far as she could tell. But that brief glimpse had given her new insight into his character and in the process had created another bond between them.

The rest of the day passed in easy camaraderie, and it wasn't until dusk that Kristina was forced to confront the fragile nature of her fantasy. When Tucker turned the car onto the driveway of a neat brick house, she felt a disquieting apprehension. He parked in front of the garage and turned toward her with a smile. "This is my home."

An odd discomfort began a distinctive flutter in her throat. "Oh, I thought we were going to the hotel."

His eyes took on a glimmer of wariness. "I'll take you there later if you want, but I was hoping you'd stay here tonight . . . with me."

The flutter dropped to her stomach. She had known that the day would culminate in his arms, but she hadn't expected to talk about it first. "Tucker, I—"

"If you'd rather I took you to the hotel now, tell me. I'll do my best to understand, but I want very much to make love to you, Kristina, and I thought you wanted that, too. If I've misunderstood . . ."

He left the question to dangle, and Kris had to answer. "No, Tucker. I want—" She swallowed hard and wondered if he had any idea how long it had been since she'd last voiced her desire. "I do want to . . . be with you tonight. It's just that I thought the hotel . . ."

Silence filled the space around her, and she wished she knew how to explain. But how could she tell him that making love in his home was too personal? God, he would think she was crazy. But it was different, more intimate, more *lasting* somehow.

By contrast, a hotel room was temporary, impersonal, a place where memories were changed with the linens. She could leave on Saturday, knowing that there would be other dreams and experiences occupying the room where she had had a brief vacation affair. But here? In his home, where he would continue to live after she was gone? In his bed, where he would awaken each morning and perhaps remember her presence beside him?

"Kristina?" He brought her thoughts full circle to his waiting gaze. "Let's go inside."

No, she reasoned, she couldn't explain, but neither could she refuse. "I'd like that," she said, and suddenly it was true.

Once they were in the house, her discomfort eased a bit, and she looked around while Tucker fixed coffee in the kitchen. His home was tastefully decorated, not too large or too small for a man living alone. Kris thought it was nice, nothing more. It lacked the character that Tucker's home should possess. It lacked focus, as if his life were actually lived in another place. *The hospital?* she wondered, and answered her silent question with a sigh. Of course. At least until John Abernathy had entered the picture.

With that thought came an unsettling comparison. Once before, Tucker's career had been threatened by a man with too much money and too little compassion—her own father. She had been both the cause of the threat and the source of Tucker's protection. Even at seventeen she had known the power of a word dropped to a college dean, so she'd borne in silence her father's demands to know Tucker's name. He'd stopped asking—and caring, she supposed—on the day she'd left his home.

Kris traced the rough weave of a tapestry on the wall and then turned, thrusting her hands into the patch pockets of her cotton skirt. So many secrets, all of them connected to Tucker.

"Coffee's on," he announced from the doorway between kitchen and living room.

Looking toward the sound of his voice, she struggled to put the memories away, to recapture the dreamy mood of the day. But it was gone, leaving only the very real pulse of need in its wake.

"It'll take a few minutes to brew." He advanced into the room, and she watched the latent power in his movements. Emptiness ached inside her; desire misted her thoughts. His expression was calm, as if he were unaware of the mounting tension. When their eyes met, though, she knew he recognized the symphony of taut nerves and breathless expectations.

"I hope you don't mind waiting," he said, his voice deep and warm, his nearness a caressing invitation.

"No." She did mind, though. Not because of the coffee but because she had waited eleven years to find him, because she had waited too long to correct a mistake that now couldn't be corrected. Her pleading protest came involuntarily from her

65

heart. "Tucker, today is Thursday. We have only one more full day together."

He offered understanding in a smile. "And two nights, Kristina." Stepping close, he placed his hands on her shoulders and drew her against him. "Two long nights."

She lifted her face to his and sought the reassurance of his kiss. In his embrace she no longer cared where they were. Here or a hotel room, it didn't make any difference. She wasn't going to forget, ever. Her first knowledge of Tucker had been colored in the rosy shades of girlish fancy. But this time—her hands slid up and over his shoulders—this knowing would be colored in the soft pastels of experiences that had transformed her from child to woman. And she wanted to remember, always.

As his lips gathered the threads of her reason and wove them into his own design, Kristina pressed against him and sighed her surrender, knowing that it wasn't really surrender at all. It was a sharing of herself, of a past of which he had been a part yet had never known.

His hands met at the small of her back and parted, each taking a different path of pleasure. She responded with the sensual exploration of his shoulders and delighted in the textured feel of muscles beneath a crisp shirt.

When he touched and then began to discover the weakness in her carefully styled chignon, Kris recognized a slow, wanton yearning drifting through her. She lifted her hand to assist his effort, and in a matter of seconds thick blond satin spilled over his fingers. With the release of her hair a husky hum of acceptance caressed her throat, and Tucker moved to capture the sound on her lips.

It was magic, splendor, a thousand longings with only one wish. Tucker and Kristina, lovers again . . . still . . . for always. When had the beautiful sense of belonging filled her? Or had it been hidden in her heart all those years, waiting for this moment?

When he loosened his embrace and stepped back, his fingers lingered against her hair; his gaze held hers with a question and a promise. In answer she placed her hand in his, trusting that he would honor her need for quiet commitments.

There would be no spoken promises. She expected none from him and would offer none herself. The night was his . . . and hers. That was all that counted. Tonight. Now. If Tucker sensed that she was more aroused, more passionately giving than perhaps another woman who was embarking on such a brief affair might be, well, that couldn't be helped. Another secret. Another mistake?

She felt a rising urgency to know him intimately, to caress him and to please him with her touch, and she saw the desire reflected in his eyes. He took her hand and led her to his bedroom. Kristina was grateful for the muted light of a bedside lamp. She was shy here, in this most private room, and she preferred to watch the shadowy silhouettes on the wall.

But her own building passion wouldn't allow her to avoid the very real image of his body—or of hers. In tacit agreement they faced each other to undress in a silence that throbbed with tension. Never before had she felt so conscious of every movement, every inch of skin, yet there was no embarrassment. There was only Tucker and the loving admiration in his eyes.

Perhaps it was an illusion, but for now she wanted to believe that it was loving, that he needed her. She had needed him for so long it seemed natural to walk, naked, to his bed and wait for him to join her.

And when he did, she gave herself up to the reality of his possession and reveled in the blending of her life with his. It was transient, never meant to last, but she was willing to bargain with the fates for the memories being created—and whatever the price, she would pay.

But the slow, sweet shivers that coursed through her seemed worth any price as Tucker cupped her breast in his hand and anointed it with his kiss. The rough-soft caress of his tongue against her skin made her aware of his tender patience and set a languorous, melting warmth adrift in her veins. Kristina moved with the current of sensual feelings and the awakening of a passion she had known long ago but that was now altogether new.

She felt small and fragile lying next to him on his bed, and her thoughts were wrapped around the mystery of her own emotions. She wasn't fragile. Her body was diminutive and slender, compared to Tucker's long, muscular frame, but she was capable of loving him with a strength equal to his. And her desire was not a fragile thing; her heart was pounding with its powerful rhythm.

His lips nuzzled the hollows of her throat and halted her trembling sigh unborn. Her hands slipped around his neck and massaged the firm set of broad shoulders. It was not enough to caress him so. She had waited too long for these precious moments; she had remembered too often the stolen hours she had shared with him so many years before. Now that he was again in her arms, warm and responsive to her touch, she wanted to take him into herself, to enclose his body with her own, and to capture his heart . . . if only for an instant.

This need to possess and to be possessed was new and a little frightening in its intensity, but oddly Kris savored the feeling. She sensed that it was an experience unique to her relationship with Tucker. He had been her first lover, the man her heart refused to forget. He had been hers for only a moment, yet her body remembered the claiming touch of his hands and responded like a rosebud in the sun.

As his mouth came to hers in a dozen sipping, clinging kisses, she pulled him down, arched against him, and whispered her yearnings against his lips. And when he moved to answer her murmurings with the moist, heated joining of their bodies, Kris knew the fiery, sweet ache of loving. She surrendered to the blending of flesh to flesh and soul to soul.

But in the soft, contented aftermath of passion she accepted the fragile nature of her emotions and knew that the price of her fantasy would be dear.

CHAPTER FOUR

The aroma of breakfast filled the kitchen on Saturday morning; thoughts of good-bye filled the silence. A buttery froth of eggs bubbled in the skillet; bacon, lean and crisp, lay on the platter; two slices of bread waited companionably in the toaster.

It was almost done. The only breakfast she would ever prepare for Tucker, and it was almost done. Yesterday they had awakened early, eaten breakfast at a nearby restaurant, and spent the day just enjoying each other. But that was yesterday. Kris touched a fork to the scrambled eggs and stirred ever so lightly, letting them cook for another minute.

Another minute. Her throat ached with each one that slipped past. Her fantasy ebbed toward memory with every tick of the clock, and she wished for another minute, and another. But it was Saturday, the morning was almost gone, and she was leaving at noon. Not a moment sooner . . . or a moment after.

Tucker walked past her on his way to the refrigerator, and she paused to savor his nearness. Without looking, without touching, she knew the texture of him: the warmth of his body; the thickness of his hair; the whispery roughness on his face before daybreak; the quick, engaging grin; the slow, seductive smile; blue eyes alight with laughter or dark with serious thought; a subtle gesture; a husky murmur. All were known to her now, discovered in the hours between sunrise and sunset, cherished in the night.

How could the time have passed so quickly? How could she have learned so much about him and yet feel it wasn't nearly enough? She watched him pour juice into two glasses, and then she turned away to scoop the eggs from the skillet to the plate. Done. Just as this interlude in the reality of her life was finished.

Tucker reached around her to push down the toaster control as his lips tucked a kiss along the curve of her neck. A sweet yearning scolded her melancholy thoughts. It wasn't over yet. There was an eternity of minutes until noon. With a sigh Kris abandoned their breakfast to pivot in his arms and return the kiss.

"Hmmm." He lifted his head after a lingering moment and pulled her closer against him. "I think I could grow fond of mornings like this. And nights like last night." His smile slanted roguishly. "And days like yesterday and nights like the night before."

An unexpected blush of remembrance fanned across her cheeks, and she lifted her palm to touch and wonder at the warmth. But the soft pleasure in Tucker's gaze made her blush feel somehow natural and feminine and right. He placed the back of his hand against her face, gliding a caress over the contours of her cheek and brushing her mouth with gentle fingertips. Desire parted her lips, and she pressed a kiss to one of his fingers, wanting to capture him in some tangible way. But he moved his hand out of reach and settled it at her waist. Then, again, he bent to soothe her lips with his.

The toaster interrupted with a loud click and Tucker turned a rueful frown to the appliance, which sat steaming complacently. "Poor timing," he announced. Kris merely smiled as she slipped from his hold and began putting things on the table. Tucker followed her example, and in a matter of minutes breakfast was ready and waiting.

As she sat across from him, taking turns with the salt and pepper shakers, the silence seemed to cluster in her throat. She hadn't said much of anything since awakening. She didn't know what to say . . . until it was time to say good-bye. Even then there would be thoughts that had to remain unspoken, so many feelings she mustn't give voice to.

She glanced at him and envied his casual movements, the way his dark shirt and jeans made him look comfortable. She was dressed similarly in denims and a knit pullover, but she didn't feel at all comfortable. Perhaps it was the unrestrained weight of her hair, usually braided and bound into a chignon as a normal part of her routine, but left free this morning to caress her shoulders in final concession to the intimacy she had shared with

Tucker. When noon arrived, it would be bound again. That was important to her.

Kris lifted her fork and toyed with the food on her plate. It had seemed important to fix this breakfast for Tucker, too. Now she wasn't sure why. She wasn't hungry, and she didn't believe he was especially so either. But it was a way of pretending, a way of postponing reality.

"Where did you learn to cook?" Tucker asked.

Her gaze met his at the offhand manner of the question. During their past two days together he'd made a concerted effort to learn details about her job, her daily routine, and her hometown. Kris had to admit he was adept at seemingly casual inquiry, but so far she'd been better at evasion.

"Ruth taught me," Kris answered, laying the fork on the plate. She traced the design on the handle with a fingertip, then absently lifted the fork again. "She owns a gift shop across the street from the building where I work, but she spends as much time in my office as her own—if not more. I suppose that isn't really so surprising, since the *Gazette* seems to be the gathering place for almost everyone in town." A warm feeling always accompanied thoughts of home, and Kris paused to enjoy it before she continued. "Ruth has been a very good friend for a very long time."

"Good friend" was hardly an adequate description. There wasn't anyone else like Ruth anywhere. Fondness brought a note of laughter to Kristina's lips. "But no matter what she tells me, I know I will never, ever be able to make piecrust the way she does."

73

"I always buy ready-made piecrust," he offered as conversation. "Of course, it usually comes with a ready-made pie as well. I get them at the supermarket. Don't you have supermarkets in . . ." He paused expectantly.

"Of course, we have supermarkets, Tucker. There just are some things I refuse to buy ready-made."

"Oh, I see. Piecrust has become a matter of principle."

Kris smiled easily, thinking how much Ruth would like him if the two of them should ever meet—but that wasn't going to happen. Her smile faded as suddenly as it had come. Ruth would never meet Tucker. Kris had deliberately avoided mentioning the town in which she lived.

When she left Denver today, her brief vacation affair would be over. She didn't intend to correspond with him in any way. Two days were all she'd offered to him, and two days were all she could steal from her own tomorrows. If she stayed another day or even a few minutes past the self-imposed noon deadline, her tightly controlled emotions would break free, and she would be irrevocably involved with Tucker, the one man with whom she couldn't risk falling in love.

Kris patted her lips with a napkin and reached for a glass of juice. Aware that Tucker watched her, she took a drink and slowly realized that she had let the conversation drop abruptly. "I'm sorry. I'm not very good company this morning, am I?"

"Maybe if you stopped trying to keep me at arm's length, conversation would come easier."

Her laugh was short and tense. "At arm's length? Is that how you describe days like yesterday and nights like—"

The look in his eyes suffocated her attempt to tease. "You know what I mean, Kristina. You're taking great pains to keep our relationship on the level of a passing affair. I've told you about my office, about the hospital, about my patients, and about the malpractice suit. You know on which days I play racquetball and what time I leave for work. You know where and when I was born, the names of my brothers and sisters, and the fact that I was once engaged to be married." His fingers tapped the tabletop with impatience as he held her gaze. "On the other hand, the things I've learned about the people and activities that fill your life number exactly three: You live somewhere in Arkansas, edit a newspaper, and have a friend named Ruth. That isn't much, Kris, considering all we've shared during the past few days."

She gazed down at her uneaten breakfast, acknowledging the truth of his observation by her silence yet knowing that Tucker knew far more about her than he realized, far more than any other man had ever discovered.

His sigh was a soft resignation. "And today you're leaving."

She looked up at that, feeling somehow defensive. "I told you in the beginning I couldn't stay longer. I thought you understood . . ." Suddenly the words she had been about to say echoed in her memory with eerie déjà vu. He had said the same thing to her once . . . on paper. She still could remember how heavy the letter had felt in her hands, how much its message had hurt. And now, with the remembering, came a feeling of sympathy. "I'm sorry, Tucker, but I must leave in a little while."

He frowned his frustration. "I'm not going to throw myself in front of your car to stop you. I'm only asking for some information: Your phone number; your address. You can't expect me to let you go without at least knowing how to find you again."

She pushed back from the table and carried her plate to the sink. "I don't want you to find me again."

His chair scraped against the tiled floor, and then his hands were on her shoulders, roughly turning her to face him. "You don't mean that," he said, his eyes intensely blue and compelling.

"Tucker, I . . ." Her self-control wavered beneath his regard, but she gathered her resolve. "You've made this a wonderful vacation, one I'll never forget. But your life, your career, are here. There isn't even a hospital in—in the town where I live. It's better if we say good-bye now and save ourselves the—"

"Tell me where you live, Kristina." It was a quiet but convincing display of his determination. The grip on her shoulders tightened, tugging at a strand of her hair and at her veneer of calm. "I'll find you one way or another, so why don't you just tell me?"

She was cornered. If she refused again, it would only make him more determined. She tried to lift her shoulders in a conceding shrug. "Maple Ridge. It's about sixty-five miles from Russellville."

His expression softened. "Thank you."

"I meant what I said, Tucker. Today is good-bye."

"And tomorrow's another day. Damn it, Kris, I'm not letting you walk out of my life!"

"You did it once before." The accusation was out before she could stop it, and she was unprepared for his reaction. He became instantly still, as if absorbing not only the words but the myriad of emotions behind them. Kris stared up at him, wishing with all her being that she had kept silent.

"My God," he whispered. "I knew someone must have hurt you at some time in your life, but I—" His hands slid the length of her arms and wrapped themselves around her cold fingers. "Am I responsible for hurting you, Kris?"

He was responsible for more than he would ever know, but the hurt? No, she had created that for herself. "I didn't mean that, Tucker. I shouldn't have said it. It was unfair to bring up the past. I'm sorry." With a wry frown she disengaged her fingers and stepped back. "I seem to be forever apologizing this morning. Maybe it's time I got ready to go."

She turned and walked toward the door, but she had to stop when she heard him call her name. Her heart pounded with futile wishes; her memory held fast to the timbre of his voice. Closing her eyes, she braced herself to face him before turning again.

"Kristina," he repeated in a voice both tender

and determined. "I don't want to spoil what's left of our time together with an argument, but I want you to know that this isn't good-bye. I have commitments here in Denver, but as soon as I can arrange it, I'm coming to see you. There hasn't been enough time to discover what kind of relationship might develop between us, given the opportunity. I'm going to give us the chance to find out." He paused as if waiting for her protest, but none would come. "I just wanted you to know, Kristina."

She nodded, and as he watched her leave the room, he admitted that the curious knot in his stomach had an element of uncertainty. Why was he being so persistent about seeing her again? And why was she so against the idea?

He didn't understand, couldn't follow her reasoning. His career was here; hers was in a small town with no hospital. What in hell did that have to do with anything? He hadn't asked her to move to Denver, hadn't considered doing so. Even if their feelings developed into commitment, as he thought they might, surely job location would be a point on which they could compromise.

He wasn't sure he had a career worthy of compromise—if the question should arise—and at the moment a town without a hospital sounded good to him. A town in which Kristina lived sounded even more appealing.

Shoving a hand into his pocket, Tucker turned to look out the window at the May sunshine. A robin poked relentlessly at the ground, and Tucker absently watched its persistence.

How had Kris become so important to him in such a short time? Two days—and two nights—had captured him, and he didn't want her to go. There was so much he hadn't discovered about her, so much more he wanted to know.

She was elusive, allowing him no more than a quicksilver glimpse of the emotion and life experiences that had created both her coolly deliberate composure and her warmly impulsive laughter. He never before had met anyone like her; he'd never before shared so much of himself with another person. And until this morning he hadn't realized that she had shared so little with him.

How had that happened? In their exchange of ideas, in the give-and-take of their companionable silences, in the communion of their lovemaking, he'd felt closer to her than he had ever felt to another person. And he'd thought she felt the same.

He frowned as the robin suddenly took flight and winged toward home. Why had Kris made that unexpected reference to the past? Was it possible that he'd been the one who'd hurt her? No, he found it hard to believe that could be true. It had been so long ago, and their time together so brief. One weekend, however perfect, was only a heartbeat in the framework of passing years.

But he hadn't imagined that peculiar edge in her voice. *You did it once before.* What had she meant? He'd been honest from the beginning of that idyllic weekend to its conclusion. He'd told her there was no place in his life for a continuing relationship, no matter how much he might wish to see her again.

The letter he'd received a few weeks later had surprised him, but he'd answered it as honestly as he knew how. And when the second letter arrived —a pale lavender envelope with a hint of fragrance; funny, he should remember that—he'd returned it unopened, deciding it was better not to allow a correspondence to develop between them. He wasn't particularly proud of his behavior now, but he couldn't believe it had created the scars that Kristina tried so hard to conceal.

He'd been a first-class fool to let her walk out of his life then. And no matter what she said, he wasn't going to repeat that mistake. The tables were turned. This time she'd told him—from the beginning—that she didn't want to get involved. But her voice, the nervous movements she sometimes made, even the shadowed look in her eyes, gave a different impression. The time they'd spent together had been as special for her as it had for him. He was experienced enough to recognize that.

But special or not, she had some reason for maintaining that elusive distance, and he was persistent enough to find out what that reason might be. He'd give her some time to gain a bit of perspective and, maybe, to miss him a little. That he was going to miss her, more than a little, was already evident. The afternoon stretched before him with all the appeal of a week-old newspaper and an empty refrigerator.

But he'd keep busy until he could go to her, see

her again, and then . . . Tucker turned back to the kitchen clutter and felt warmed by the memories of their morning together. For the first time in almost a year he felt good about life and about himself. Kristina was an inseparable part of that emotion, and he wasn't going to let her slip away without a protest.

When she walked into the kitchen again a few minutes before noon, Tucker had sorted through his thoughts and decided to treat this good-bye as the temporary parting he intended it to be. But seeing her hesitate in the doorway, as if she, too, were dreading the coming farewell, tested his resolve to keep things casual.

Her hair no longer covered her shoulders in fine-spun gold. It was confined now. It was no less beautiful, simply different. Just as the expression in her eyes was different. Solitude was almost a tangible part of her again, and he knew she had her emotions under strict control. She looked calm and reserved, ready to leave Denver—and Tucker McCain—behind.

He waited there by the window, wanting to go to her and hold her close for a while. But he waited instead, hoping she would make the gesture and come to him. She took a step. He breathed again, and when she placed her hand in his larger one, Tucker thought he had never known a feeling quite so special.

"I'm going to miss you, Kris." He spoke lightly, knowing she would shy away from anything more. "You haven't left yet, and I'm already feeling a little lonely."

Her smile was fleeting and noncommittal, but he saw the wistful reflection in her eyes. "I wouldn't like to think you could forget me too soon, Tucker."

He squeezed her hand and then bent to brush her lips in denial. Her mouth was cool and moist to the touch, but he didn't press for a response. Not yet. "I won't do that, Kristina. I'm planning to write your name on my arm in case I have trouble remembering."

Her gaze flew to his in startled surprise, and then her smile made a slow, laughing reappearance. "I'm going to miss you, too, Tucker Mc-Cain."

"Well, keep your mind on the map this afternoon. I don't want you to get lost between here and Arkansas. You can miss me when you stop for the night. You can lie in bed and think of me lying in bed thinking about you. And, Kris"—he moved his hands to rest on her shoulders—"I want you to call when you get home. I need to know that you're safe."

A quiet pleasure swirled inside her at his concern. "I'll call."

He drew her into the circle of his arms, and she linked her hands at the back of his neck, holding him close, savoring the last minutes of his nearness. Their eyes met and held, sharing the knowledge of what had been and an awareness that it was ending. Kris lifted her lips in invitation, wanting to forget in the sweet enchantment of his kiss.

Tucker met her halfway, and his touch brought a rush of warm emotions. The sense of belonging made a slow spiral through her thoughts as it did every time he held her. Lips, hands, body, soul, she was his for this one eternal moment. All that she had to give she gave to him, and she knew it was only a fragment of what she wanted to give. But she wouldn't think of that now.

With gentle insistence she aligned her thighs to seductive closeness with his. Her breasts ached with wanting his touch, and she curved her fingertips into the dark, soft thickness of his hair. She wished for more time, for another hour to spend in his arms, in his bed. She wished for a future unblemished by the past, and she wished with all her heart that she didn't have to say good-bye.

But it was over. She drew back, her mouth clinging to his in reluctant parting. There was a tender yearning in the blue gaze that caressed her face; there was a muted promise in the way he traced the outline of her mouth with his fingertip. She closed her heart against that promise, not willing to acknowledge or deny its existence. "I have to go now," she murmured, her voice thick with the words she would not release.

He took her hand, and they walked through the silent house, stopping only long enough for Tucker to pick up her suitcase. That seemed final somehow, and Kris lifted her chin in acceptance.

Outside, the sunshine was cheery bright. The air held a nip of mountain freshness and the evanescent aura of spring. Kris always took her vacation in spring, or at least she always had. She thought perhaps she might choose a different season of the year next time.

Her shoes made a scuffy whisper against the sidewalk; Tucker's made no sound at all. Her Ford gleamed bronze and almost new in the driveway, holding its own against the glistening black Mercedes beside it. She was glad now that she'd checked out of the hotel yesterday. She had kept her car in the hotel parking lot all week, but yesterday she had brought it here when they had gone to get all her things. At least she wouldn't have to fight the downtown traffic again.

Kris stopped beside her car and waited as Tucker took the key and went to place her luggage in the trunk. A robin hopped across the lawn and paused, alert to the presence of intruders in its domain. The slam of the trunk lid sent the bird winging to the nearest tree in startled flight, and Kristina smiled, directing Tucker's attention upward when he came to stand beside her.

"Friend of yours?" she asked.

"Just a nodding acquaintance. I don't believe he realizes he's intruding."

"He's probably thinking the same thing about us."

Tucker slipped his arm around her shoulders and turned his smile to her. It faded slowly into sobriety. "Stay with me, Kristina."

The husky plea stabbed deeply into her control, and her heart pounded with sudden regret. "You know I can't."

"Why?"

She dropped her gaze to shield her own weakness. "Don't ask. Please. I . . . Really, I have to leave. It's been . . ."

"Wonderful, I know." He moved to open the door for her. "Spare me the 'thanks for a memorable vacation' line, all right?" He held the door as she got inside. "Just don't forget me, Kris. Don't even try."

She winced as he slammed the door, but then, impulsively, she was rolling down the window and reaching for his hand. It felt large and comforting to the touch. "Tucker?" He leaned closer to hear her. "I really hate good-byes."

His palm cupped her cheek, his lips claimed hers, and then, all too soon, he stepped back. He withdrew his hand from hers, slowly, deliberately prolonging the touch of fingertip to fingertip for another minute . . . and another. "Be happy, Kristina DuMont."

And then it was over. She started the car, put it in gear, and glanced over her shoulder before backing out of the drive. She lifted her hand to wave, but Tucker wasn't watching. He was looking up at something in the tree. She supposed he was watching the robin, and she felt a ripple of disappointment that his attention was already focused elsewhere. She didn't look back again. Instead, as she drove away, she glanced at her watch. It was five after twelve, and she was on her way home.

At the first stop sign she groped for the map and the piece of paper Tucker had given her and found them beside her on the seat. Good. She shouldn't have any trouble. A sudden sadness misted her eyes, and she blinked quickly to clear her vision. How silly to cry now. She'd had a wonderful vacation. She had some wonderful memories. She was going home. *Be happy, Kristina Du-Mont.*

She stared hard at Tucker's bold handwriting and then concentrated on following his written directions. A right turn. A left. Two stoplights. There. The highway signs indicated the road leading away from Denver. Away from Tucker.

She had taken this road before, she thought as she turned the car onto the highway and increased the speed. Then it had stretched in endless miles between Columbia, Missouri, and St. Louis, but still it had led away from Tucker. And she'd had no idea where that road would ultimately take her.

Kris fidgeted with the tight coil of hair at her nape, trying to adjust it to comfort. She should have told him good-bye, though. She should have made herself end, once and for all, what she had recklessly begun eleven years before. In a few days, a few weeks at most, the time she'd spent with Tucker would assume a dreamlike unreality, and he would be a part of her past, as he had always been. Still, she should have said that final good-bye.

What if he followed through on his stated intention of finding her? Had he meant what he'd said about giving their relationship the time and opportunity to develop into something more? No, she didn't believe he had. In the span of a relatively short time she knew she would be nothing but a memory to him . . . again. He would be caught up in the demands of his career within another month. She would bet on it. The "time and opportunity" simply weren't going to come.

Be happy, Kristina DuMont. His parting words returned, and she tugged at the pins in her hair. She had known little real happiness in her life, but she knew contentment and was grateful for its steady pattern. Maybe that in itself could be considered a measure of happiness.

The pins came free, and her hair tumbled about her shoulders, delighting in the wind that whipped through the car window. Immediately Kris wondered why she'd released it and then, just as quickly, understood. It was an admission that she was not the same person she'd been a few days ago. She'd known from the moment she saw his name in the newspaper that he could change her. Hadn't he done it once before? So many years ago. So many roads crossed since then. But in the final analysis hadn't *everything* in her life changed because of him? And hadn't his life taken the exact road he'd carefully planned . . . because of her?

Determinedly Kris closed the window and turned her whole attention to the highway. She had miles to go before the feel of his mouth, the touch of his hand, the curve of his smile faded to memory. There were miles and miles of highway ahead of her, but home drew nearer with every one. And she wanted to be home.

If only she'd said good-bye . . .

CHAPTER FIVE

"What do you mean, you just decided to drive straight through?" Ruth Barnett lowered her bifocals to the end of her nose and directed a reprimanding gaze over her wire rims. "My God, Kris, that's a fourteen-hour drive."

"Eighteen, actually, if you don't count—"

"You generally have better sense. What possessed you to . . ." Ruth paused, slowly taking off the glasses as she perched on the corner of Kris's desk. "You met someone, didn't you? By God, you finally met someone. What's his name?"

Kris leaned back and tapped a pencil on the tattered arm of her chair, as if her thoughts were a million miles away. They weren't, but it never paid to respond to Ruth's questions too quickly. Kris had discovered that if she waited long enough, sometimes Ruth even spared her the trouble of answering at all. Not so, today, apparently.

"New skirt, Ruth?" she observed dryly. "Nice color. You must have gone shopping while I was on vacation."

Ruth smiled and smoothed a crease into the

khaki fabric. "You were with me when I bought this *years* ago. Come on, Kris, tell me the whole story."

"Don't you need to check on business at the shop? How can you leave your employees alone for hours at a time?"

"I hire dependable, competent people who manage to turn a profit without my continual presence. Now, what's his name? And what did he do to send you home in an eighteen-hour gallop?"

Reaching down, Kris pulled out the bottom drawer of her desk and propped her feet on the edge. Then she clasped her hands in her lap, keeping the pencil between them for support or defense, she wasn't sure which. "His name is Tucker McCain. He lives in Denver, and he didn't *send* me home. I left."

The green eyes widened; the bifocals paused in midswing. "Good Lord, Kris, do you mean he wanted you to stay? And you *left?*"

"Thanks a lot, Ruth. Whatever happened to 'Welcome home, Kris. Good to have you back'?" Kris shook her head. "Do you know not one person in this entire newspaper office has said that to me this morning? I walked in the door a little while ago—two days before I'm supposed to be back from vacation—and passed Gary on his way out. Do you know what he said, Ruth?"

"I don't care what he said, Kris. Let's get back to the man in Denver."

Kris frowned her exasperation and ignored the interruption. "Gary took one look at me and said, 'Where the hell have you been? The computer's down, and the post office is on fire. Of all the Mondays for you to oversleep!' Before I had a chance to defend myself, he was gone—to the fire, I assume—so I came in here and phoned the repair service. Back to work as usual. I should have stayed in bed."

"Well, don't expect any argument from me. After driving all the way from Denver without a stop, I'm surprised you could even drag yourself out from under the sheets, much less think about coming to the office." Ruth placed a hand flat on the desktop blotter and leaned down in a confiding manner. "Why *didn't* you stay in bed, Kris?"

"I wasn't tired. I slept for hours after I got home yesterday. I couldn't sleep anymore." That was true, Kris assured her conscience. There was no point in telling Ruth or anyone else about the dreams that had awakened her at intervals during those hours or about the way her heart had pounded in protest when she'd reached sleepily for Tucker only to realize she was alone. "And I never said I drove for eighteen hours without a stop."

"That is completely beside the point. It isn't like you to risk your health, not to mention your car, in a marathon race. And I've never known you *willingly* to come into work on a day you didn't have to." Ruth smiled in smug omniscience. "Now, what happened with the man in Denver?"

Kris tossed the pencil to the desk in surrender. "I met him, and we went to dinner, did some sight-seeing. Nothing spectacular, but it was nice."

"Nice?"

With a sigh she met Ruth's persistence squarely. "It was wonderful, but it ended, as all vacations must. He lives there. I live here. Period."

"From where I sit, that sounds like a question mark. Don't tell me you left without getting his phone number?"

"I have his telephone number, complete with area code." Kris restrained the impulse to check her slacks pocket and to hold the piece of paper in her hand again. She'd already worn her thumb-print onto the corner and memorized the thick black strokes of his pen. She had meant to call him the minute she'd arrived home. But for some reason she hadn't.

She had waited, told herself he wouldn't be expecting a call quite so soon. Hadn't she told him she planned to take her time, drive to Arkansas at a leisurely pace? But once on the road, she hadn't wanted to stop, and she'd simply kept driving. Still, she should have phoned him. Maybe she had procrastinated because she wanted him to wonder, to know what it was like to wait for a call that never came. Kris sighed in soft resignation. She would call him this morning, but not until Ruth left the office. And that might take some fancy fabrication. "Ruth, I have the number, but I'm not going to call him."

"Well, write, then. Send a note thanking him for your wonderful vacation."

Sitting straight, Kris shoved the bottom drawer closed with her foot. "I hardly think a thank-you note would be appropriate, Ruth."

There was a sudden stillness. Kris rubbed her

temples and wished that she had stayed home. But she'd been restless, unsettled. There had been thoughts, memories, what ifs and if onlys following her through every room in the house. She'd thought it would be better here at the office. She'd thought she wouldn't see Ruth until later. She'd thought she could put Tucker from her mind.

"Is he married?" Ruth's voice dropped to a hoarse growl. "My God, you didn't get involved with a married—"

"I'm not totally inept, Ruth. Give me credit for having at least a little sense."

"If he's not married, then I don't see the problem."

"That's because there isn't one."

Ruth twisted her bantamweight body from the desk and stood, regarding Kris somberly and placing her bifocals on the top of her head in deliberate dispute. It was a gesture Kris knew well, and she firmed her chin in reply.

"We've been friends a long time, Kristina. If you don't feel like talking about your *wonderful* vacation, that's fine with me. But if you ask my opinion, I think it's about time you stopped punishing yourself for a mistake you made a thousand years ago. Risk a little hurt for a little happiness." Ruth pursed her lips and then softened them with a rueful smile. "Sorry for the lecture. Melinda called from college last night, and I guess I didn't get all the mothering out of my system."

A change of subject. Kris breathed a silent

thank-you. "How is she? Will she be home for summer break?"

"Yes." Ruth rubbed the back of her head and walked to the office door. "I don't know why that makes me happy. In less than three weeks I'll have more laundry, no phone privileges, and limited use of the car. There's something convoluted about our educational system. You should write an editorial about that, Kris." She started through the doorway, then paused to take the glasses from her head and place them on the bridge of her gamin nose. "Why don't you do that right after you make the call to Denver?"

Kris smiled sweetly. "And why don't *you* take a hike?"

"My, my." Reddish brows arched in amused surprise. "The high altitude in Colorado must have thinned your sense of humor. Would you like to come over for supper tonight?"

"Not unless you're offering to do my laundry."

"Let's make it tomorrow night. That'll give you time to get the film developed so you can show me a picture of Mr. Wonderful."

"His name is McCain. Dr. Tucker McCain."

Ruth took a step back into the room. *"Dr.? As in General Hospital?"*

Kris nodded, and Ruth shook her head slowly. "A doctor, Kris. The one thing Maple Ridge needs more than cable television, and you left him in Denver. I honestly thought you had better sense." She held up a hand and backed from the office. "All right, all right. Not another word. I'll see you tomorrow."

The doorway stayed empty for all of ten seconds —Kris counted—before Ruth returned with bifocals in hand and a warming smile. "Welcome back, Kristina. I'm glad you're home."

This time Ruth left, and the doorway remained empty. Kris propped her chin in her palm and tried not to feel tired. It was a losing battle, one she had fought ever since leaving the Denver city limits on Saturday afternoon. Somehow all her vitality and enthusiasm had stayed behind—with Tucker.

But she would get it back. Maybe a little more slowly than she would like, but if nothing else, the years had taught her to accept the waiting. Ruth had never understood that. She was a mover, wanting to change what she didn't wish to accept. *Risk a little hurt for a little happiness.* How like Ruth to issue such a challenge and how like her to dismiss "one" mistake as if it had happened a thousand years before.

What would Ruth say if she knew how a few days in Denver had complicated that original mistake? No point in wondering, because she wasn't going to know. Contrary to what Ruth might believe, any and all discussion about Tucker was closed. Almost.

Now that she'd told Ruth, there was only one more thing she had to do. Kris slipped a hand into her pocket and withdrew the crumpled notepaper. She stared at it for several long minutes before she lifted the telephone receiver and dialed. Her heart was a frantic flutter in her rib cage as the phone rang and rang. Trembling, she had started to replace the receiver when she heard the click and the ringing stopped. God, what was she going to say? Think. Swallow. Hold the phone steady.

But there wasn't any need, she realized within the empty space of sound. Tucker wasn't answering his phone; his answering service was. Disappointment welled inside her, and she covered it with the rational argument that talking to his service would be easier all around. No deep emotional inflections in his voice or in hers. No need to convey any feeling at all. Just leave a message. *Tell him you arrived safely. Tell him everything is all right. Tell him . . . good-bye.*

That wasn't so difficult, Kris thought as she finally put the telephone back into its cradle. Now the loose ends were gathered. Now her life could get back to normal. Now she had told him good-bye.

A buzzer seared the air with its angry hum, and Kris answered the intercom. As she put the phone to her ear, she searched the desk drawer for a pad and pencil. Vacation or not, the *Gazette* office stayed the same. Today Kris appreciated that fact. Business as ususal. Probably the only thing on earth that would help her forget Tucker McCain.

Considering that she'd spent the entire afternoon in the hot July sun, it really wasn't surprising. Hallucinations often accompanied heat stroke, she believed, and the shiny black Mercedes had to be a mirage, although it looked heart-stoppingly familiar, parked in front of Ruth's gift shop.

It had been six weeks, specifically six weeks, four days, and several hours, since last she'd seen a car like it. Kris had a strong impulse to brake in the middle of Second Street and take a closer look. But with city hall and the Maple Ridge police station only half a block away, she thought it better to park her own car before she investigated another. Besides, there had to be hundreds of black Mercedes in the world. To assume that this particular one could belong only to Tucker was absurd and— Kris glanced over her shoulder as she drove past— all too reasonable.

She turned the steering wheel sharply, and the tires bumped the curb as she pulled into a parking space in front of the *Gazette* office. Kris was out of her car almost before the engine had idled to a stop, her gaze crossing the street to search the Mercedes for some identifying mark.

The license plate was angled out of her line of vision, and there was nothing unusual about the automobile itself, except that it was here. Few Mercedes of any color found their way to Maple Ridge, and fewer still parked downtown and across the street from her office.

Tucker was here. The knowledge was closing around her like the humidity on a sultry summer day. Without going any closer, she knew the Mercedes belonged to Tucker, and an unbidden rebel welcome flowed through her veins. Her lips curved in momentary anticipation and just as quickly tightened with uncertainty.

She should have been prepared for this. Kris knew she'd wrapped herself in the illusion that he wouldn't come, that she wouldn't be faced with the questions this day would bring. Because he hadn't phoned or written or tried to contact her in any way, she'd decided he had realized that their brief affair had no future. And she had accepted the disappointment as well as the way she still reached for him in the night.

Her gaze swung slowly to the double glass doors of the newspaper office. Was he inside, waiting for her? Or was she imagining the possibility that he cared enough to follow her, to give their relationship time and opportunity to develop into something more?

And even if it was true, what then? Kristina straightened her shoulders and reached inside her car for her notebook and camera. She could cross only one bridge at a time.

In the reception room of the *Maple Ridge Gazette* Kris noticed an unusual lack of activity. Of course, there were any number of reasons for Effie to be away from her desk, but the sound of voices and laughter from down the hallway suggested an impromptu party. Nor was that in itself uncommon; the town's residents looked on the newspaper office as community property and the one place where if you stayed put long enough, you were bound to see practically everyone else.

With a frown Kris started in the direction of the noise but paused before a small, round mirror on the wall. She checked the condition of her chignon and the silk bow tied at the collar of her striped blouse. Both hairstyle and bow showed definite signs of drooping, and Kris revived them as best she could before continuing down the hall to her office doorway.

She stopped there, aware of the presence of her co-workers but conscious only of Tucker. He was leaning against the edge of her desk, arms crossed over the wine-colored shirt he wore, legs covered in denim and stretched in casual, effortless support. His hair was tousled and dark, his skin tanned and smooth, his smile friendly . . . until he caught sight of her. Then, in a wondrous moment of greeting, his smile softened with sensual gladness and became a sweet reminder of his kiss.

Kristina braced a hand against the doorframe in sheer self-defense. Her breath was a shallow pressure in her lungs, her pulse was a wild flutter in her throat, and she couldn't stop the pleasure that rippled through her time and again. Tucker was here, near, touchably close. But she mustn't touch him. She simply couldn't walk into his arms as if nothing beyond a yard of floor space separated them. And she wouldn't satisfy the curiosity of her friends by displaying her most private feelings.

But oh, she wanted to touch him. So much so that she forced her gaze away from him to the other occupants of the room. Ruth, glasses anchored in the clustering red curls atop her head, perched on the corner of the desk closest to Tucker. Gary, owner and publisher of the *Gazette*, sat in one chair. Effie, the dark-haired secretary-receptionist, sat in the other. Matt Saradon, mayor and the town's only practicing attorney, stood in the middle of the room with his back to Kris.

She cleared her throat, and Matt turned. "Hello, Kris. You've got company."

Her brows lifted, but she didn't reply.

Ruth filled in the gap. "Don't worry about making introductions. We've already introduced ourselves."

"And given Tucker a rundown on local news," Matt added.

"And gossip." Effie stood and adjusted the belt of her calico print shirtwaist. "We didn't tell him much about you, though. We figured you'd need something to talk about when you got here."

Effie's chuckle was accompanied by a round of smiles and amused nods. Kris met Tucker's eyes across the room, and her discomfort at being the object of collective teasing faded. Somehow she felt that he understood and enjoyed the affectionate camaraderie of this group of friends.

"Did you get the feature story?" Gary asked, a grin hiding in his dark, bushy beard. "What was it this time? A giant radish?"

Kris again tugged her gaze from Tucker and tried to gather her scattered thoughts. "Nothing so exciting. A bumper crop of watermelons. But I think there's a good human-interest story—"

Gary interrupted with a groan and levered himself lazily to his feet. "Surprise me, Kris." He held out a hand to Tucker. "Nice to meet you. I hope you'll stay around long enough for us to take that fishing trip I mentioned."

"Thanks, Gary," Tucker said with a smile and a handshake. "I'd like that."

Matt stepped forward to extend his hand to

Tucker. "You'll have to come over for supper one evening. Jena and I live just down the street from Kris." Matt turned to include Kristina in the invitation. "Maybe next Saturday would be a good time."

"Saturday?" she repeated ambiguously as she wondered how to postpone an outright refusal without sounding completely tactless. Apparently Matt took her acceptance for granted and proceeded to enlarge the original invitation to include everyone present and several people who were not.

Kris moved away from the doorway, intending to circle the discussion group and put the space of a cluttered walnut desk between Tucker and herself, but she found herself caught in the shuffling good-byes of well-meaning friends. Before she could take steps to prevent it, she was beside him, looking up at his half-amused, half-frustrated expression, matching the quiet yearning in his eyes with a soft ache of her own.

She was vaguely aware that the room was clearing and that the hum of conversation was moving into the hallway, and she knew that in another minute she would be in his arms. Pivoting abruptly from the temptation, she laid her camera, purse, and notebook on the desk. "Hello, Tucker," she said with false nonchalance. "What brings you to Maple Ridge?"

"Do you know you're the first person to ask that?" He leaned against the desk again and regarded her thoughtfully. "Everyone else immediately assumed I came to see you."

"And did you?"

His hand reached for hers, and though she didn't encourage it, her fingers nestled against his as if they belonged there. "You know why I'm here, Kristina."

She sighed her uncertainty. "I really didn't expect to see you again."

"That isn't what Ruth led me to believe." Tucker smiled and pulled Kris closer to his side. "She was talking to Effie when I walked in this afternoon, but the minute I introduced myself and said I was looking for you, Ruth practically sang the 'Hallelujah Chorus.' "

"But instead she said, 'By God! You're the doctor from Denver. Where in the hell have you been?' "

"Something along that line," Tucker said. "It went more like 'Kris and I thought you'd never get here.' "

Kristina shook her head. "Ruth is a good friend, except for those times when she tries too hard to be a good friend."

"You're fortunate to have people who care as much about you as Ruth and the others obviously do. For a while there this afternoon, I was afraid I wouldn't pass muster. Everyone was a little cool toward me until they decided my intentions were strictly honorable." His arm went around her waist, and Kris realized how cozy they had become in a matter of minutes. It was too easy with Tucker. Talking, the sense of closeness—it came too easily, and she had to stop it from going any farther.

She slipped from his loose grasp and walked behind the desk, fortifying her resolve by the distance she'd placed between them. "Just what are your intentions, Tucker?"

He turned slowly to face her, his eyes dark with questions, his jaw firm with determination. "I told you before you left Denver that I wasn't going to let you slip out of my life. Maybe it's too soon to talk about commitments, Kristina, but—"

"Yes. Yes, it is too soon, Tucker." Her voice had an edge of panic. "And it's going to stay that way."

"I don't think so," he said slowly, the very softness of his tone underlining his sincerity. "And that's what I'm here to find out."

She faltered, unable to think of an effective argument, regretting the impulsive actions that had brought her to this confrontation with her past. "What about your medical practice? You can't be away from it indefinitely."

"My career is on hold at the moment. That's another reason I'm here. I'm not sure I want to return to medicine . . . ever." He held up a palm at her immediate protest. "I just don't know, Kris. There are some things I need to think about, some decisions I'm going to have to make. And while I'm thinking, I'd like to be with you. You seem to understand my ambiguity better than I do, and I need someone in my life who understands." His fingers curled into a fist of frustration. "God, that sounds so damn selfish, doesn't it?"

Kristina closed her eyes against his emotion, but her heart refused to shut him out. He needed her. The lawsuit had shaken his self-confidence, had left him needing something and someone to believe in. And at the moment he was looking to her to provide both. Oh, yes, she did understand, only too well. "Sometimes, Tucker," she said in a voice thick with memory, "sometimes the only way to survive is by being selfish."

"Maybe I phrased that wrong." He walked around the desk, and his hands cupped her shoulders to turn her gently into his arms. "Maybe I should have said I need *you*, Kris. And I believe you need me just as much. Surely there's more to life than surviving."

She didn't want to acknowledge that possibility. For years she had managed to avoid it, but now Tucker was here, his touch warm and inviting, and she knew she couldn't delude herself any longer. Once she had wanted desperately to be needed by someone, anyone. Wasn't that the real reason she'd gotten involved with Tucker so many years before? Hadn't she simply wanted to feel necessary to another person? And he had filled that need, if only for a weekend.

This time he needed her, and as he bent his head to brush her lips with tenderness, she thought how easy it would be to get lost in being needed by Tucker. The kiss deepened, his embrace tightened, and her body responded with a wild and wondrous desire. But Kris knew she must stop the sweet seduction before she forgot the reasons she had to end it.

Pulling back, she braced her palms against his chest and braced her courage with a deep breath. "Tucker, please. I didn't mean for this to happen. I never intended to mislead you, but I truly thought you understood that the end of my vacation was also the end of our affair."

The corners of his mouth creased. "There haven't been a lot of women in my life, Kris, but there have been enough for me to know that this is not an affair. And it isn't over. For almost two months I've thought about you, missed you, and ached with the memory of holding you. I didn't phone or write because I hoped you might be missing me as well. And I wanted to arrive unexpectedly and maybe surprise you into an honest reaction."

He released her from the shelter of his arms, but he continued to hold her by the steady blue of his eyes. "When you first walked into this room and saw me, you weren't thinking in terms of an affair that had already ended, Kristina. You were glad to see me. Maybe a little uncertain but glad just the same. Now, are you going to tell me that was a lie?"

"No, that was honest, Tucker. And so is this: I don't want you to stay. Right now you're disillusioned with your career, with life in general, but it won't last forever. In a few weeks you'll be ready to give your first love—medicine—another chance. You'll go back to Denver or to some other place, and you'll rebuild your practice because being a doctor is important to you. This"—Kris indicated their surroundings with a gesture of her hand—"is important to me. I'm happy here, and I don't want you to change that."

"Am I really that much of a threat to your peace of mind, Kris?" He touched her cheek with a questing fingertip. "How can you think I would ever hurt you? I only want a chance to love you."

She didn't flinch or even look away at the words, but her heart pounded a painful reminder against her ribs. Tucker had no idea of how threatened she was by his very nearness. If he stayed, she would be risking much more than a little hurt. She stood to lose everything.

She was already half in love with him, and a few days, a night in his arms would steal her heart completely. Once he possessed her love, it would be only a matter of time before he asked for a commitment, and then she would have to tell him about the baby.

And what if someone else told him? The possibility made her pale. Too many people in this town knew the circumstances that had brought her to Maple Ridge. What if someone mentioned to Tucker—No, she knew that wouldn't happen. That the idea had even occurred to her was a measure of her anxiety. In this close-knit community there was an unwritten code of loyalty, a deep respect for another person's privacy. No one would willingly violate her trust. If Tucker learned the truth, it would be because *she* told him.

Turning, she took a step away from him, knowing that when he knew what she had done, he would hate her. And she couldn't bear that. It had been better before, a thousand times better when she hadn't known where he was or what his life was like. She had been secure in the knowledge that what he didn't know couldn't hurt him, that she alone bore the responsibilities and the regrets.

She sensed his presence, felt the warmth of his body behind her, and wished she could take refuge in his strength.

"Trust me, Kris. Just a little."

His whisper mingled with the soothing touch of his hands on her shoulders, and for a moment she weakened. "I have an extra bedroom. You can stay tonight, as my guest. But tomorrow . . ."

He looked as if he might object, but then his lips formed a determined smile, and only the shadows in his eyes betrayed his inner perplexity. "Won't it cause some . . . talk if I spend the night in your house?"

Her mouth curved ever so lightly. "Not nearly as much as if you didn't."

"I can see I have a lot to learn about life in a small town."

"Yes. Well, I have to get this story written before I can leave the office. Why don't I give you the house key and you can make yourself at home?" She moved to the desk and wrote her address on a piece of notepaper before she rummaged in her purse and produced the key. "I'm sorry I can't be a more gracious hostess, but—"

"Let's don't muddy the water with polite insincerities," he interrupted with a sudden cool edge on his voice as he took the address and the key from her shaky fingers. "Finish your story. I'll find something to do." He walked to the doorway and stopped. "And if I'm not there when you get home, check the mailbox for the key, and don't bother to wait up."

Kris stared after him, listening to the sound of

his footsteps in the hall. She heard him say something indistinguishable and recognized Ruth's voice answering. Kristina sank onto the worn cushion of her office chair and rested her head in her hands. Ruth had probably eavesdropped on the entire conversation and would have plenty to say later on the subject of good sense.

With a sigh Kristina reached for her notebook and began to leaf through the pages.

CHAPTER SIX

Tucker heard the sound of her car on the graveled drive. It seemed as if he'd been listening for hours, but it couldn't have been much more than thirty minutes since he'd returned from Ruth's house. It had been barely nine o'clock then, and the sky had been a dusky rose twilight.

It was dark now. The night had come while he wandered aimlessly through the rooms of Kristina's home. His self-directed tour hadn't taken long—a stop in the doorway of each room, a glance to note color and furnishings, and a closer look at the personal touches that told him a little something about Kris.

But there was nothing to explain her less than encouraging welcome that afternoon or the way she'd left him on his own for the entire evening. If it hadn't been for Ruth, he might have been on his way back to Denver by now.

Tucker folded his hand around the chain that anchored the porch swing and waited for the hum of the car engine to stop. Kristina would be with him in a few minutes, and the thought made him oddly nervous. She didn't want him to stay. She was afraid that if he did, she'd be hurt. That much he understood, but her reasons for being afraid? He was at a loss to explain those. He'd given her no cause to believe he would love her and then leave her the moment his life settled into perspective.

All right, he would admit her observations about his career were astute. His disillusionment with the medical profession would undoubtedly fade with time, but he knew he had reached a crossroads. Maybe the lawsuit had only precipitated the restless feeling that there was something missing in his life. Regardless of what had brought him here, he was at a turning point. And Kristina had a part in his eventual decision, whatever that might be.

The slam of the car door carried clearly in the July night, and he tensed, setting the swing in motion and then halting it with a push of his feet. What would he say? Why had he decided to stay when she'd made it clear he was only a guest? A temporary guest. Fewer than two months ago he'd been more than that, much more. And today in her office he'd have sworn the look in her gray eyes, the subtle trembling of her hand in his, the controlled yearning in her kiss were those of a woman greeting her lover.

He heard her footsteps and the sound of the back door opening, then closing again. He listened to the rustle of noise, vague but audible, as she moved through the house, pausing at intervals—to look for him perhaps? The night seemed suddenly, inexplicably filled with maybes and possibilities. He might be risking a rejection of devastating proportions, but he couldn't leave without trying to discover why Kristina was afraid of him or of making a commitment . . . or possibly both.

She opened the front door and hesitated behind the screen. The light from the living room cast her silhouette in a golden shadow, and Tucker felt his throat tighten with her nearness. Never in his life had he wanted so badly simply to *be* with another person.

"Hi," she said softly. "It's still very warm outside, isn't it? Would you like something cool to drink?"

"No, thank you. I had something very cool at Ruth's just a short while ago." Tucker slowly released his grip on the chain and tried to lessen the tension in his voice. "She told me I was drinking home brew, but I have a feeling it came straight from Kentucky."

Kris pushed open the screen door and stepped out onto the shadowed porch. "You went to Ruth's house?"

Was he imagining a nervous edge in her tone? Did she think he and Ruth had spent their time discussing her? Tucker frowned at the thought of how little information he'd actually gleaned during the past few hours. Ruth was glad he was here, and she was certainly encouraging him to stay, but her loyalty, first and last, belonged to Kris.

"All in all," he answered lightly, "it was an interesting evening. When Ruth found out you were working late, she insisted I join her for dinner. But first I had to meet the salesclerks at her gift shop. Then, since it was 'just around the corner' and 'right on our way,' we stopped at the bank and she introduced me to any and all personnel who hadn't managed to escape before we arrived. There was a stop at the market for bread, milk, and an introduction to the store manager."

A low laugh drifted from Kristina to capture him with its evanescence. "You should have asked her what happened to her regular chauffeur."

He smiled as he watched Kris move closer. "I didn't have a chance. Somewhere between stops there was a really pitiful story about being deprived of transportation and leisure activities by someone named Melinda."

"Who happens to be her daughter and the source of an inordinate amount of parental pride." Kris leaned against the porch railing. The light from inside the house touched her hair and face with pale illumination. "Ruth has a son, too. Michael. He recently graduated from college and took a job in Little Rock."

" 'With a company that hires only the top graduates in the nation.' When it comes to that parental pride, Michael has equal billing with his sister."

"I hope Ruth didn't bore you with scrapbooks and home movies."

"No. How anyone could use the term 'boring' in connection with that little lady is beyond me. She makes me feel criminally lazy."

Kristina was silent for several long minutes as she stared at something in the starlit darkness. "Michael and Melinda are . . . adopted. Did Ruth mention that?"

"No." Lifting his arm to rest along the back of

the swing, Tucker wished she would come sit beside him. "Did you finish the story?"

"What?" She looked puzzled and then nodded her understanding. "Oh, you mean the human-interest article. Yes, it's ready for tomorrow's paper."

Silence again. A stilted what-do-I-say-now sort of hesitation hovered in the summer air. Tucker released his breath in a muted sigh and thought about saying good night.

"I owe you an apology," she said in a reluctant voice. "It was inexcusable for me to leave you on your own this evening. The story really had to be written, but I could have gone in early in the morning to do it. It was just that I—" Her fingers began to trace a spiraling pattern along the wooden railing. She watched the movements, and Tucker watched her, wanting, *aching* to offer comfort for the distress he sensed in her but couldn't name.

When she straightened and turned to him with a casual smile, he knew the vulnerable moment had passed. Kristina lifted a hand to the knot of silvery blond hair at the nape of her neck, and Tucker wondered if she wore the controlled hairstyle for the sake of coolness or for the restraint it represented.

"Aren't you uncomfortable in this heat?" she asked, all trace of uncertainty gone from her voice. "It must be very different from a summer night in the Rockies."

"Yes, but for some reason I'm enjoying the heat, humidity and all. It reminds me of Fourth of July

112

fireworks and homemade ice cream and playing softball until after dark and walking barefoot over wiry summer grass. Do you have a hoard of childhood memories like that, Kristina? Things you never think about except on nights like this?"

Kris looked back to the starry coverlet overhead and felt a wistful pang for the simple pleasures that she had missed as a child . . . and for the memories she would never share with her own child. "I grew up believing that ice cream came in prepackaged scoops ready to be served in a crystal dish and that summer was created by parents so they could send their children to camp. God, I used to dread the end of the school term." She paused, remembering. "It really wasn't as bad as it sounds. All things considered, I suppose I was happier during those summer camp sessions than at almost any other time in my childhood. And I know my parents were."

"Kris." Tucker spoke in a sort of surprised hush, and she heard the creak of the swing as he stood. His footsteps sounded hollowly against the porch floor. He stopped a couple of feet away from her, to perch on the edge of the railing. "You surely don't mean that."

She lifted her shoulders in a dismissing shrug. "I never learned a great deal about softball at camp, but I saw some terrific fireworks displays."

"Would you like me to tutor you in the fine points of sandlot softball?"

Such a gentle, easy tone. Kris loved him for accepting her reticence to discuss a less than cherished past. She hated her weakness in giving him

113

even that small glimpse of an old hurt. "It's a little late in the season for that, don't you think?"

"We have the rest of the summer."

Tensing, she turned toward him. "But you're leaving tomorrow."

"No."

"Tucker, you know . . ." She couldn't continue. He watched her too closely, held her gaze with the honest blue of his own eyes.

"I know that you *assumed* I would, but I can't leave yet, Kris. Already I feel comfortable in Maple Ridge, and I like the people I've met. Matt wants to talk to me about the possibility of building a hospital here. Gary invited me to help him snare an elusive bass. The manager of the grocery offered to show me around his family's orchard. Ruth tempted me to dinner tomorrow night with a promise of fresh peach cobbler." He glanced out at the quiet street and patted a thoughtful rhythm against his thigh. "I'm staying for a while, but I won't impose on you. I'll find another place . . . an apartment, maybe."

"No." The protest was automatic. To think of his *living* nearby, seeing him during the course of her days, wondering about him at night, hearing friends ask the same curious questions again and again—No, she couldn't bear to have him so close yet distanced from her. Maybe here she could convince him of her sincerity. Maybe she could discourage him from staying too long. Maybe she could face her own selfish conflict in wishing he could stay for so much longer than "for a while."

She inhaled a deep, supportive breath. "There's

114

no need to find another place, Tucker. You're . . . welcome here. I'm gone quite a bit of the time, and if you've decided to spend a few days in Maple Ridge, you may as well stay with me."

"Thank you, I believe I will."

Her gaze locked with his in a moment of wary alert, but he returned her searching look with unguarded candor. She couldn't be sure what he was telling her in the silence, but she knew he was gradually tightening his hold on her heart, testing the strength of her resolve, and tempting her to forget the very thing she must remember.

Tucker smiled easily and stood to extend his hand to Kristina. "Why don't you show me where the guest bedroom is located? It's late, and I'll confess that I'm a little tired."

She knew she should restate her position again, make certain he understood that their relationship wasn't going to progress any further. Yet her hand was reaching for the pleasure of his touch. It was another mistake to add to a growing list, but as she walked beside him across the porch and into the house, Kris couldn't find the courage to correct it.

Jena and Matt Saradon lived on a rambling farm that was a little farther down the street than Tucker had at first imagined. Three miles from Kristina's front door to the Saradons' mailbox was Tucker's best guess, but he didn't think anyone cared enough to measure. Distance was a relative term in Maple Ridge, just as "neighbor" was gauged more by a communal affection than close proximity.

The "neighborhood" was well represented in the Saradons' backyard on Saturday night when Tucker and Kristina arrived. The drive to the farm had been the closest he'd been to Kris for more than two days, two busy days in which he'd learned a lot about the community and very little about the woman who was temporarily sharing her home with him.

It was discouraging, Tucker decided as he swallowed the last of his iced drink and set the glass aside. Across the bricked patio Kristina chatted with a laughing group of her peers. He was surrounded by a more serious group and a conversational topic of deep importance to the men discussing it. Tucker had little concentration or advice when it came to the subject of a community hospital. The only subject that aroused his interest at the moment was Kristina and her subtle aloofness.

She caught his gaze and smiled, lifting her glass in a silent gesture of acknowledgment. The last rays of the sunset brushed her hair with amber and tinted her complexion a honeyed rose. His throat tightened at the delicate features, the softly arched brows over eyes that veiled her thoughts and feelings the way a mist conceals the morning. She was dressed in lightweight cotton slacks and a blouse that was knotted intriguingly at her waist. Her lips formed a warmly sensuous curve, and he could see little sign of aloofness. But he knew it was there, waiting, maintaining a distance that he simply couldn't understand.

At least she hadn't asked him to leave again, and she didn't seem to mind the energetic welcome extended by her friends. Tucker realized that his supposed relationship with Kris was responsible for the warm acceptance bestowed on him, but he saw no point in trying to set the record straight. Who would believe him anyway? Anyone with a remnant of romanticism could tell he was in love with her.

Tucker reached blindly for the glass he'd set on a nearby table and closed his fingers around the sweaty sides. It was too early for an admission like that, especially when she tried to discourage him at every turn. Yet he knew that time would only prove it true, and even then convincing Kristina that he knew his own heart would be a formidable task.

Still, time was on his side, he reasoned, and he could legitimately find a number of good excuses to prolong his stay in Maple Ridge . . . and in Kris's home. The main possibility was being debated at that very moment by the three men standing with him. The subject of building a hospital was near and dear to the heart of every citizen in town.

Tucker wasn't sure what he had to offer other than a professional viewpoint, but Matt had asked him to help, and he'd agreed to do so. Getting involved in the community had not been in his original plans, but it now seemed tantamount to being involved in Kris's life. And one way or another he meant to accomplish that.

"Would you like something else to drink, Tucker?" The husky feminine voice drew his gaze and his attention. Jena Saradon, petite, dark, and engaging, smiled up at him.

"That would be great." Tucker stepped back to let the continuing conversation close ranks. He'd been listening only peripherally to the men anyway, and he wasn't sorry for the interruption. "I could use a little more ice, and maybe I'll try the lemonade this time."

"Then, by all means, follow me." Jena started toward the house. Tucker fell into step beside her, shortening his strides to match her unhurried seven-month-pregnant walk. The pregnancy didn't seem to slow the light, inconsequential chatter that she utilized, as a hostess often does, to put a newcomer at ease. Tucker saw no reason to tell her he already felt more than comfortable. He enjoyed talking with her, liked to watch the sparkle of contentment in her brown eyes.

It was hard to believe those eyes had known tragedy, but Kristina had told him that the Saradons' first child had died. An accident had happened here on their farm, too far from the nearest medical facilities. Little wonder that Jena and Matt were determined to get a hospital built in Maple Ridge. The wonder was that they actually thought he could help.

In the neat kitchen Jena refilled his glass and handed it to him with a statement that sounded oddly like a question. "I asked Kris how long you were planning to stay in town."

"Oh?" Tucker sipped at the tart lemonade. "And what did she tell you?"

"That you'd be leaving in a couple of days." With a frown Jena leaned against the Formica countertop. "Matt thinks you'll be in Maple Ridge until the new hospital is dedicated." Brown eyes settled on him with disquieting regard. "Would you like to know my opinion?"

He acknowledged his interest by a slight arching of his brows and hid the sudden caution filtering through his body.

"I think you could be happy here indefinitely. I know it's presumptuous to hope you might prefer practicing medicine in our small community over a larger, more well-endowed position somewhere else."

"Well-endowed?"

His smile couldn't be camouflaged, and Jena responded with a laugh. "You know what I meant. Besides, that isn't the point. Staying in Maple Ridge is." Her hands laced together as her voice softened in earnest. "We need you here, Tucker. We need your help in building the hospital, and we need dedicated professionals like you to staff it."

"Jena, is there any lemonade left?" Kristina's question preceded her into the room, but thirst became of secondary importance as her gaze met Jena's determined expression and then drifted to Tucker. A shaky sensation threatened the backs of her knees as his lips curved in a welcome.

"Come in, Kris," Jena said. "There's plenty of

119

lemonade. Help yourself; then you can help me persuade this doctor of yours to consider the career potential our community has to offer."

Her whole body stilled in quick discretion, and then Kris managed a casual laugh as she moved to replenish the liquid in her glass. "I'm sure Dr. McCain has heard enough persuasive arguments for one night." An ice cube clinked against the crystal. It had a false ring, just as her unconcern rang falsely in the words she said. "Nothing I have to say would add to your cause, Jena. Tucker is a surgeon. It's understandable that he would prefer to practice in the city."

Jena's eyes widened in surprise, and Kris turned her back and her attention from the two other occupants of the kitchen. She wished she hadn't offered a comment. Already she knew the direction of Jena's thoughts; already she could imagine the whispers that would circulate before the evening ended: *A lover's tiff. She wants him to stay. He won't leave the city. It'll work out, though. Kristina has good sense. . . .*

The pitcher of lemonade tilted dangerously with the thoughts, and Kris frowned as the cool drink spilled over the rim of her glass.

She reached for a towel only to discover that Tucker already had one in his hand. As he dried the wetness from the counter, she wondered why she believed small-town life was so great.

"Don't listen to her, Jena." He rubbed briskly, his tone easy, self-assured, and unthreatened. "Kristina's being modest. I think she might be able to persuade me . . . if she set her mind to it, of course."

"Well, then I can only hope she sets her mind to it." Jena straightened and brushed a maternal hand across her extended waistline. "Now maybe I should rejoin the party and see if anyone else is dying of thirst." She started for the door and glanced back. "Are you two coming with me?"

"Yes." Agreement came swiftly on the heels of the question, and Kris noted the subtle arching of dark brows—both Jena's and Tucker's. But she didn't care. The community she loved, the friends she trusted, were backing her helplessly into a corner, taking Tucker's side in the mistaken belief that it was her side as well. "Let's go," she said brightly, and proceeded to follow her hostess from the house.

Jena stepped outside, but Tucker caught up to Kris just before she walked out the doorway. "You're in a terrific hurry, Kris. Planning to scotch the rumors about us before they have a chance to circulate? It's a lost cause, you know. Half the people here think I'm courting you, and the other half believe you're courting me, and they're all hoping one of us succeeds."

She looked up, wishing the underlying vein of seriousness were merely his way of teasing. "Because they want a doctor for the hospital, Tucker."

He shook his head in dispute. "It's because they want you to be happy, Kris. And as best I can tell, you're the only one present who doesn't believe I can make you happy."

"You're very arrogant to suggest that, Tucker."

121

"Aren't you being a little arrogant in denying that the possibility exists?"

She tipped her chin in cool restraint. "We're wasting time, Tucker. Let's join the party."

He reached past her to push open the back door. "All right. We'll drop the discussion, but remember that simply because something has ended doesn't mean it's over."

No, she decided as she moved onto the patio with Tucker's warmth right behind her. It wasn't over. And if tonight was any indication, the best she could hope for was a postponement. Her feet seemed to be planted in the wrong direction, and even if they weren't, there would be a crowd of Maple Ridge residents ready and eager to give her a push in Tucker's direction.

Over? She had a feeling the tug-of-war had just begun.

CHAPTER SEVEN

July scorched into August with record-breaking temperatures and monotonously clear skies. Summer, always a slow season for the *Gazette,* was almost bereft of newsworthy events. Deadlines came and went with very little urgency or excitement. It was simply too hot to generate interest in anything other than the weather forecast—with one notable exception.

The community hospital made the front page of every issue of the biweekly newspaper during those long, hot weeks. For some reason that no one could explain, the disputed issues began to resolve themselves into progress. Final plans were made and approved; financing became available through a private endowment and a federally funded loan. Maple Ridge residents rallied, despite the heat, to borrow, beg, or steal the rest of the money needed. And through the sometimes arduous process, Tucker was given credit for every success.

He was quick to deny that his "opinions" had any real significance in resolving the problems, but no one doubted the value of his counsel or his ability to unite factions. It had been slightly less than two months since he'd taken up residence, yet there already were indications that Tucker was becoming a part of the community, a valued member in his own right. And he was becoming a part of Kris's life as well.

Quietly, one day, one evening at a time, he fitted himself into her routine. He was there in the mornings to share with her a companionable silence and a cup of coffee before she left for work. Occasionally he dropped by the office to sit amiably chatting with Gary or Effie while his smile warmed Kris from a distance. Some evenings, when nightfall produced a cooling breeze, they sat side by side on the old porch swing, talking or not saying a word, close in thought or thinking of things a world apart, never touching in even the most casual way and yet aware, completely aware of the pleasure touching would bring.

If Tucker was discouraged with the platonic nature of their relationship, he kept the feeling well hidden. Kris knew she didn't fare as well when it came to concealing an inner conflict that grew more serious for her with each day. Torn between wanting to keep her heart safely out of his reach and enjoying and beginning to need the serenity of his company, she couldn't convince him that she wanted him to leave Maple Ridge. She often mentioned his imminent return to Denver, but Tucker ignored the hints and kept his own counsel, giving no indication of when or if he meant to leave.

There wasn't a doubt, however, in the minds of

Kristina's neighbors and friends. Tucker McCain was proving himself to be a worthy member of the community and, of course, he would stay. It was time that Kristina settled down with a good man, and Tucker was certainly that. Besides, he was a doctor, and he was helping build the hospital. It was obviously a match made in heaven—for Kris and for the community.

Kris hated hearing the rumors that ran rampant through the town and inevitably found their way to her as thinly veiled, good-natured teasing. She hated even more the thought that Tucker was hearing the same rumors, but no amount of denial could slow the friendly speculation. She and Tucker were a "couple," a team working together for the betterment of Maple Ridge. Although no one had as yet brought up the subject of a wedding, Kris knew the question was heading in her direction.

As the days edged toward September, it became evident to Kris that she'd waited much too long to correct the situation. No one believed her when she insisted she and Tucker were just friends. No one even listened when she stated that he wasn't going to stay in town and take charge of the new hospital upon its completion. Kristina realized it was pointless to argue. There was only one person who could negate the rising expectations and restore a sense of perspective to an increasingly awkward situation. And somehow she would convince Tucker that he had to do just that.

It wasn't the best way to begin a weekend—especially when it was the first one she'd had free in weeks—but then there wasn't going to be a perfect time to confront him with the rumors. Still, maybe Sunday afternoon would be better . . . No, she had delayed too long already.

Kris tossed aside the tangled sheets on her bed and decided to face Saturday morning and Tucker all in one brave sweep. He would be in the kitchen now, with a mug of steaming coffee and the Little Rock daily paper. He always awakened early, before her alarm shrilled the beginning of another day. It was a habit born during med school and strengthened by the hospital's surgery schedule, he'd admitted once. It was one of the few references he'd made to his career during his stay in her home. She had learned very little about *Dr. McCain*, but she had learned much about Tucker, the man.

She knew, for instance, that he read the newspaper from page one to the end, skimming at times but never skipping an article. He liked his coffee hot and black and at leisurely intervals throughout the morning. He enjoyed quiet times and being with her; to her memory no one had ever seemed so happy or so content simply to have her nearby. Kristina touched her lips as she thought of the way he smiled each time he saw her, a soft, secret smile that made her heart feel like a kite tripping foolishly over a cloud.

With a sigh Kristina pushed herself into a sitting position and ran lazy fingers through her tousled hair. Tucker was too much at home here, and she, well, she was too much at home with him. It was going to be lonely when he left. Her house would

126

never feel the same again; it couldn't belong totally to her anymore. Nothing would be the same, not her home or the community or her friends . . . or herself.

But this wasn't the time for such melancholy thoughts. She needed a cool, brisk shower to clear her head and focus the words she wanted to say. She needed to wash and dry her hair, and she really should take a few extra minutes to dress in something more formal than her usual shorts and top.

God, what difference did it make what she wore? That would only be postponing the inevitable. Kristina pushed her feet to the floor and made herself stand beside the bed. The shower was essential for her composure, but everything else could wait.

Tucker was not in the kitchen, she discovered some twenty minutes later. He wasn't even in the house, and with a frown she wished she *had* taken time to wash her hair. There was a sense of anticlimax as she sat drinking a cup of coffee alone, and she couldn't help wondering where he'd gone and how soon he'd return.

The questions stayed with her throughout the day along with a mounting frustration. When Tucker finally arrived just after dusk with a freshly filleted bass and a big grin, Kris wasn't in the mood to hear a recount of his fishing trip. For some reason she couldn't quite define, she was edgy, wanting the situation with Tucker settled but not knowing where to start. For hours she had imagined the conversation, and now, when he was finally facing her, the words were tangled and elusive in her mind.

"You'll have to come with us next time, Kris." He walked from the back door to the refrigerator and placed the catch of the day inside. "Gary has a cabin not ten yards from the creek where we fished. It was unbelievable." As he straightened, his grin flashed briefly toward the kitchen doorway where she stood. "I wish you could have been there today when—"

"I wish you'd left a note. I had no idea where you were, Tucker."

The refrigerator door closed slowly, and Tucker's eyebrows rose in careful question. "Is something wrong? Were you worried?"

"No. I just wanted to . . . talk."

"All right."

She released a shaky breath and made another attempt to gather her scattered thoughts, but composure evaded her grasp. "Maybe I should take another shower first," she said with a slight smile.

His leisurely smile slanted with a tender amusement. "Isn't that supposed to be my line?" He lifted his hand to indicate the faded clothes he wore. "If this were a contest to determine who gets first turn in the bath, I'd win hands down. You look as fresh as cow's milk." He grimaced. "God, I'm beginning to speak the Maple Ridge dialect. Definitely time for a shower."

"Then we'll talk," she said, finally finding a steady voice.

"If that's what you want." He moved toward

her, and Kris backed away as he approached. His expression creased with concern as he noted her defensive steps, and he stopped beside her, his hand lifting tentatively to her face. "What is it, Kristina? What's wrong?"

His palm felt warm against her cool cheek, and the woodsy scent of sunshine clung to his skin. She looked into his eyes and knew the exquisite ache of desire. She could taste the sweet memory of his kiss on her lips, remembered the hard symmetry of his body. Helplessly her tongue skimmed the contours of her mouth. "Tucker, I . . ." Kris stopped, and her sigh trembled between them. "I'll wait for you in the living room."

He nodded a puzzled agreement and left her standing alone in the hallway.

It was only a little more than a quarter of an hour before he joined her in the living room, but she'd had enough time to bolster her composure. Not quite enough time, though, to be prepared for the sight of him clad in Levi's and nothing more. Her gaze went to the cluster of dark curls on his chest, dropped to his bare feet, and rose again to meet his eyes before continuing upward to the damp disarray of freshly washed hair. He rubbed a towel haphazardly over his head and smiled in his quiet, special way.

"Sorry, I know I'm underdressed, but I got a little too much sun today. You don't mind, do you?"

This wasn't fair. Without a word he'd put her at a disadvantage. His manner, his total lack of tension, the confident curve of his mouth under-

129

mined her self-control. He didn't look sunburned. He looked . . . wonderful. And her senses throbbed a message to her brain that had nothing to do with wanting to talk.

Taking her silence as acquiescence, Tucker advanced farther into the room and stood behind the sofa. He continued towel-drying his hair as he watched Kristina turn to face him. Her expression mirrored the calm of a summer sky, but her eyes were stormy gray.

"I suppose you've heard the rumors," she said tentatively.

He slowed the movements of the towel. "What rumors?"

"About you. About . . . us."

"Don't tell me someone's been *gossiping* about us, Kris." He lightened his tone with a hint of teasing but waited in vain for her smile.

"You know what's being said as well as I do, Tucker." An edge of exasperation found its way into her voice, and she half turned away from him. "Everyone thinks you intend to stay here and work at the new hospital."

"And?"

A frown threatened the corner of her mouth as her gaze went to his bare chest. A sudden longing tightened her throat and didn't ease when she raised her eyes to his. "And they're saying that we"—she hesitated momentarily—"are well matched."

"I can't take exception to that, Kris. I think we're almost a perfect match, don't you?"

"This is serious, Tucker. It isn't right for you to

stay in Maple Ridge any longer. Already you've raised expectations that you can't possibly mean to fulfill, and—"

"That has the ring of an accusation. Have I raised *your* expectations? Is that what this is all about?"

"No! I'm talking about the people of this community, *my* neighbors and friends."

"Mine as well."

"Only because of me."

Damn! His temper began a slow rise. "You don't have a monopoly on friendships in this or any other town, Kris."

"But I'm not the one who's allowing *my* friends to believe I'll be the new hospital administrator."

He clenched his irritation into the folds of the towel and then let it slide to the floor. "I have no intention of becoming any kind of administrator no matter what the entire population of Maple Ridge cares to believe. I'm not sure I even want to be a doctor. But I know for damn certain that I'm not going to stand here and defend myself. I haven't lied to anyone in this town, least of all you."

She brushed a sweaty palm over the tan fabric of her slacks. "I don't think you've lied, Tucker. I think you're raising unfair expectations when you let the townspeople believe you're planning to become a permanent resident."

"And I think you're being unfair when you assume I won't choose to do exactly that."

"You don't mean that."

"Is it inconceivable to you that I might want to

131

live here? That I could enjoy the kind of life you enjoy?" His heart flinched at the look of panic on her face and at the visibly trembling fingers that touched her lips and then the knot of braided hair at her neck. In that instant of utter quiet Tucker recognized a raw physical need to possess her, to take advantage of her vulnerability, to strip away the careful façade and make her admit that she cared.

"You can't stay in Maple Ridge, Tucker," she said in a stilted whisper. "It would make everything so . . . difficult."

The intensity of his desire blurred into a burning sensation in the pit of his stomach. "Why?"

She pivoted to the window, rubbing her hand over the sill, hiding her thoughts from him, and suddenly he crossed the distance between them and turned her to face him. Wide gray eyes stared up into his, and the longing to kiss her almost overwhelmed him. Instead, he tightened his hold on her shoulders. "Tell me why, Kristina."

"I told you from the beginning that you shouldn't expect anything more from me than friendship."

"And have I?"

"Yes! You expected me to—to fall in love with you, to be your lover."

"But that hasn't happened, Kris, has it?"

"No, not—" She caught herself before she said what she felt, but his heart heard her qualification and began to beat a faint rhythm of hope. "It isn't going to happen either," she continued. "I won't let myself become any more involved with you than I am at this moment."

"And how involved with me are you?"

She floundered at that. He could see the distress in her expression and knew that she was preparing to deny any involvement at all. He spoke first to prevent her lie. "After all, rumor has us practically married. I'd say that's pretty involved, wouldn't you? Have you been raising unfair expectations among your neighbors and friends, Kris? Or do I take the blame for that as well?"

"Don't, Tucker. I'm only trying to discuss the situation with you."

"You're trying to do something, Kris, but discussion isn't the right word for it. Are you looking for an argument? An excuse, maybe, to get me out of your house? If that's what you want, just say so."

She bent her head, and Tucker stared down at the gossamer sheen of her hair. God, how he wanted to weave his fingers into the shiny blond strands. He wasn't leaving this house, no matter what she might say.

"I want to end this, Tucker." The words came low and muffled, and he leaned close to hear. "The rumors, the expectations, everything. You're the only one who can do that. Please, Tucker, let it end."

Maybe if he hadn't been standing so near to her, maybe if she hadn't lifted her face to his as she made the almost desperate-sounding plea, maybe then he would have tried harder to understand. But with the silken caress of her breath on his skin, he couldn't think, didn't want to analyze. Not when there was a simpler, more tempting interpretation waiting on her lips.

Heart pounding, all hesitation gone, he lowered his mouth to hers, felt the tremor that coursed through her at his first gentling touch and knew he loved her. Completely. Without reservation. As the kiss deepened, his arms closed around her slenderness, and his love opened to draw her irrevocably into his soul's embrace. Her hands lay passively against his chest for only a moment before they slid up and around his shoulders to hold him as he was holding her.

This then was the end of it, he thought. This wild, tender explosion of sensation was the end of falling in love and the beginning of much more. This was the end of the tension, the wary courting. It was the end of expectation and the dawn of reality. *Kristina.*

Tucker. A husky murmur of longing floated to her ears, and Kris wondered if she had spoken his name aloud. She wanted to; she wanted to hear the rhythmic sound of it, wanted to taste the wonder of his name on her tongue. But she would not separate herself from him, not willingly, not again. This was the end of her resistance. She had neither the strength nor the will to fight a love that had begun long before this moment of acknowledgment.

She was in love with Tucker. There would not be an end to that. Even now the feel of his skin against her fingertips seemed a pleasure she had always known, as familiar to her as the touch of morning sunlight. And she welcomed his return to her arms with the same sweet acceptance.

Her lips clung to his tenderness; her thoughts clung to the truth dawning within her. She had believed his leaving would end her conflict, would return her life to its normal pattern. But she had deceived only herself. Tucker had known how she felt. He had understood the emotions, the words she hadn't said. And he had ended the lie with the honesty of his kiss.

"Kristina." It was a rough whisper of warmth against her cheek, a soothing promise to the wild, pulsing beat of her desire. His lips flitted feather-ingly along the curve of her chin, lingered at the corners of her mouth, touched her nose, her eye-lids, her temple, stole her breath, and then re-vived it with his own. He retraced the design until she was weak with wanting him, until she had no strength for anything but the loving.

Her hands caressed him, murmuring a silent message of admiration and urgency over the pow-erful slope of his shoulders. His body was so muscu-lar, so smooth and firm, and she wondered at the gentle pressure of his embrace, which made her feel safe and cherished and small, yet she was aware that he was surrendering as much to her as she was to him.

She touched him freely, allowing her fingertips and her lips, to know and communicate the full extent of her exquisite delight. This was the morn-ing of their love, and she wouldn't turn her face from its warming glow. It might be transient, fleet-ing, offering only a short span of sunlight until the secret night would separate them. But she could not turn away.

She fitted into the symmetry of his masculine angles as if she had been formed for that purpose. And perhaps she had. Tucker seemed to take that intriguing possibility for granted. His hands cupped her hips, aligning her against him with a firmness that left no room for doubt.

When his lips discovered the sensitive hollows of her neck, Kristina found the roughly soft covering of hair on his chest and eased her fingers into its damp tangle. Shivers of wonder wrapped themselves around her, and the empty feeling inside her became a slowly burning need.

With a low, throaty murmur of longing Tucker lifted his head and looked into her eyes as he began to coax the buttons of her blouse apart. It was a leisurely persuasion that held her motionless, almost breathless, in a world that consisted solely of blue eyes and a gentle touch, a world that belonged only to her and to Tucker. She was lost in the enchantment, lost to all but this new knowledge of a love shared. For that was the true magic —the love that had grown despite her wish.

It shouldn't be. It was rooted in a past that stretched cloying tendrils into the future. Yet she felt the sweet innocence of the existence of this love that she had never hoped to know, never dared dream he might share.

The fabric of her blouse slipped away, and her skin tingled with the pleasing awareness of his gaze. Kristina didn't know or care how he undressed her; she was conscious only of wanting him to do so. She offered encouragement with slow strokes of her palms from his shoulders along the corded muscles of his arms to his wrists and then back to the beginning point. Desire was a melting sensation deep within her.

When at last she was clothed only in his admiring look, she lifted her hands to her hair. In a matter of seconds it tumbled about her shoulders, a cascade of disheveled silver and gold, a symbol of the emotion she wanted to voice, the intimacy she wanted to know.

There was a seductive shyness in her movements as she lowered her arms and waited for Tucker's response. It wasn't intentional, simply a result of her own disquieting passion, a realization that no matter how many times he had made love to her, this was different.

The words, the spoken confirmation were an intangible part of this joining. She sensed that he was savoring the silence, waiting to tell her how he felt, just as she was testing the weight of her own emotion, trying to shape it into syllables. She didn't really believe "I love you" would be said by either of them for a while. It was too newly discovered, too unfamiliar, too special. And Kristina knew that once said, it would bring irrevocable changes to them both. But she would tell him when the moment was right. No matter what had happened in the past or what would happen in the future, Tucker deserved to hear her say it.

He removed his clothes and held out his hand to her. She accepted it without hesitation, going to him and lifting her face to his. For long, quiet seconds she stood waiting for the kindling stroke of his kiss, wanting, needing to feel the texture of his masculinity against her skin. When he bent his head and his breath mingled with hers, Kris gave up the waiting. She pressed into the shelter of his body and captured him in her arms.

Together they sank to the carpet and began the timeless ritual of caressing and responding to the sensual pleasure of each other. His hand at her ankle made a tantalizing foray upward. His lips at her breast heated the ache in her stomach to a fevered passion.

When he shifted his weight and filled the emptiness inside her, Kris cried out softly at the sweet tenderness of their union. Tucker was gentle, and she loved him all the more because he gave each kiss, each rhythmic movement a special touch of love. But as desire crescendoed and enveloped her in a trembling, building need, Kris wanted the driving force of his strength to consume her. She wanted to lose herself in his embrace.

Then, in one, glorious, splendid, perfect moment, they experienced the essence of their love, and she knew she was forever lost in its beauty.

CHAPTER EIGHT

It was difficult for Kristina to awaken the next morning. Something was pressing in on her, weighting her dreams with a heavy apprehension. Kristina struggled to escape the shadowed, sluggish world of sleep. Her breathing quickened, then steadied as she began to recognize the familiarity of her bedroom: same patterned wallpaper; same dark oak dresser and bed frame; same butterfly-print sheets.

She rubbed her foot over the bed linen and felt the warmth of Tucker's body beside her. Even the same lover as the night before. Her lips curved gently but never quite formed a smile. How odd that already he felt familiar in her bed. But then hadn't he become the most familiar part of her every day?

Turning her head, she looked at the dark hair, mussed by sleep and her own loving touch. His face was relaxed and still, his lips pale against the contrast of his morning beard. Eyes closed, he dreamed on, and she watched, remembering other awakenings in his arms, wondering how many more there would be.

Kris held back a sigh as her gaze moved to the window, to the light stealing past the curtains and into the room. The carpet looked almost white in the concentrated pool of sun. Its natural beige color was visible in a wide patch of uncluttered floor before it darkened to a shadowed brown in the corners. It was Sunday, and her choices seemed to have the same shaded pattern as the carpet.

What was she thinking? There wasn't any choice for her, any more than there was a true variance in the color of the carpet. Only the lighting, the perspective, made it appear different. And she had lost the privilege of perspective. She had forgotten the reason for all her careful rules, and she had let herself fall in love with Tucker.

He stirred, then settled again, and emotion rocked her heartbeat with a soft, sweet tenderness. *Let herself?* She had been helpless to prevent it. And now she had to face the reality that her fantasy had formed.

Slowly, so as not to disturb him, she eased herself from the bed and stood looking down at him for several quiet minutes, savoring the solitude and the intimacy of watching her lover sleep. He belonged here with her. She acknowledged that truth just as she accepted the fact that he would not stay.

Pivoting, she walked silently into the adjoining bathroom and splashed cool water on her face. She rubbed her skin to rosy life with a towel, and then, with deliberate intent, she forced her gaze to the mirror. Dusky-lashed gray eyes stared back at her, and she combed a hand through the untidy strands of pale hair. She eased the arch of one slim brow with her fingertip, but the mirrored reflection would not release her from its hold.

Once, on another Sunday morning, she had stood before another mirror, searching for outward signs of change. Had it really been only eleven years? It seemed an eternity since she had been so young or so foolish as to believe that life could be seen in a piece of silvered glass.

There was no need to search her reflection today. She knew the changes that Tucker had brought. Her attitudes, her routine, even the way she thought about tomorrow—he had changed them all. On that other Sunday she'd had no idea of what lay ahead—decisions, responsibility, maturity . . . a child. Dear God! How was she going to tell him that he had a daughter? Somewhere.

Kris had thought she could face anything. On the day she signed the adoption papers and kissed her baby good-bye, she had believed she would die from the hurting. She had wanted to die, but time had patched the scars and mended the pain to a soft, aching emptiness. Somehow she had survived.

But now she had to tell Tucker, and suddenly that seemed much worse than anything she had ever had to do. To say the words, knowing the shock, the hurt, the frustration he would feel . . .

The conflict churned inside her and would not be soothed. Why had she gone to that courtroom to see him? Why had she opened a door that should have remained forever closed?

Kristina reached for a brush and began pulling it through her hair. The bristles were rough against her scalp, but the woman in the mirror displayed no sympathy. The eyes that stared back at Kris were clear and steady without a hint of uncertainty. The brushstrokes slowed and then ceased altogether.

It was time to stop making excuses. She had brought about the situation that faced her now, just as she had created the situation all those years before. She had lied to Tucker by the very silence which she had used to protect him. But hadn't she really been trying to protect herself? Wasn't it possible that she had gone to the courtroom that day not out of simple curiosity but for a much more complex reason? Had she wanted to see him, touch him, love him because he was the only link she had to her child?

Abruptly she turned her back and closed her eyes to the thought. It wasn't something she wanted to consider, but it had to be acknowledged. Before she faced Tucker with the truth, she had to confront her own motivations, her own feelings. She had to know beyond a doubt that her love for him was pure and honest, an emotion separate from the past.

"Kristina?"

Tucker called to her from the other room, and her heartbeat quickened with a gentle wonder. She knew in that moment, in the husky thrill that rippled through her, no amount of self-examination would change the fact of her love. Whatever her subconscious reasons for seeking him out after

142

so many years, he was a part of her life *now*. She loved him *now*.

With hairbrush still in her hand, she made a slow turn and offered one final excuse to the mirror. *A few more days won't make any difference. I'll tell him . . . soon.*

"Kris?" His call came again.

"Coming." She tucked the brush into the drawer, aware suddenly that time—once her trusted friend—was pressing in on her, weighing her down with its passing. "Soon." She whispered the promise aloud and then deliberately avoided her reflection as she left the room and went to be with Tucker.

"Gary said we could have the cabin for the weekend." Tucker dropped the information into the darkness and felt Kristina go tense beside him on the bed.

"Oh. That would be nice, but I have so much to do at the office this—"

"Gary also said you could have the weekend off."

"Oh." Her hesitation was almost tangible. "Well, in that case wouldn't you rather go to Hot Springs or some other wild, exotic resort?"

Tucker shifted onto his side and bolstered his slightly elevated position with the pillow. "I'd rather be alone with you. That's why I suggested the cabin. It's quiet, and we'll have an opportunity to talk away from newspaper deadlines, neighbors who drop by, and telephones that ring at the most inconvenient times."

"What's the matter, Dr. McCain? Is small-town life getting to you?"

There was a teasing lilt to her voice, and he could see the faint curve of her lips, but there wasn't a smile in her eyes. Even though her expression was hidden from him by the twilight, he knew there wasn't a smile. For days now her gaze had been a confusing shadowy gray. "The only thing that gets to me is you, Kristina DuMont. I thought surely you'd caught on to that by now." He lightly stroked the bare skin on her stomach. "How much convincing do you need?"

"Lots." Placing a palm against his cheek, she leaned up and kissed him. His arms went around her shoulders to give support, and the banked embers of desire sparked a low, throbbing heat deep within him. And then, too soon, she was pulling away, her lips lingering with a soft, less than satisfying apology. "But no more tonight. I've got to be at the office early in the morning. Tomorrow noon is—"

"Deadline," he interrupted, holding back his sigh of frustration. "I know."

"Tucker, I'm sorry. But now that school's in session again and construction is under way on the new hospital, there're a lot of community activities that have to run in the *Gazette*. We've been so busy I'm surprised Gary would even consider giving me the weekend off. You must have twisted his arm pretty hard."

"I figured the time alone with you would make the effort worthwhile. I didn't think it would be quite so difficult to convince you."

144

Her laugh was a bare ripple of sound. "Don't be silly. There's nothing I'd like better than spending the weekend alone with you."

"Good, because we're leaving early Saturday morning. Now . . ." He bent to tease her lips with a kiss that promised a thousand delights and then withheld all but one. Her arms went around his neck as she sought to capture more, but he lifted his head and smiled at her expressive sigh. "Go to sleep, Kris. You need your rest."

"Damn you, Tucker," she whispered. "That wasn't fair."

"Plan your revenge for Saturday." He lay back against the pillow, wishing he felt as lighthearted about the coming weekend as his tone implied.

"You can count on that." There was a pause, and then, beneath the sheet, he felt her fingers seeking a hiding place within the warmth of his hand. "You *are* counting on it, aren't you, Tucker?"

"Actually I was thinking about how much fishing I could work into two days."

"In that case I'll be sure to pack my tackle and lures."

"You can forget the lures. One good tackle ought to do it."

Silence came, holding within it the essence of laughter, the communion of shared thoughts. Yet there was a shadow—a shadow that eluded his understanding no matter how he tried to grasp it.

"Tucker?" she whispered, her voice blending with the soft stirrings of the night. "Thank you."

His hand tightened over hers. "For what?"

"For planning this weekend. For the past few

days and the wonderful long nights. For making me see that there's more to life than surviving." She hesitated, and her tone dropped to a husky low. "I'm glad you came to Maple Ridge, and no matter what . . . Well, I just wanted you to know that I am glad you came."

His first impulse was to ask her what in hell she was trying to do to him with her half-finished comments of "no matter what." It wasn't the first time she'd begun a sentence only to let it fade into a riddle that he couldn't fathom. His second impulse, more tempting than the first, was to get out of bed and have a riddle-solving drink of Ruth's home brew.

He did neither. He simply held Kris's hand and wondered why he felt apprehensive. More to the point, he wondered why *she* felt apprehensive about him. He couldn't understand that at all, but he knew it was true because he recognized the subtle nervousness that belied her outward calm.

Did she think she would awaken one morning and find him gone? Was that the source of her uncertainty? Or was she afraid of trusting the emotion, the commitment that as yet remained unspoken? He might have told her how he felt days ago if only she hadn't shied from even the slightest reference to a serious discussion. It was almost as if the subject of love and marriage were forbidden to them, yet in the past week he hadn't come close to discovering why.

He was counting on this weekend and the quiet surroundings of the cabin to help him discover the answers. Kristina loved him. He couldn't be wrong about that. There was such a gentle look in her eyes when she thought he didn't see, and her response to his lovemaking was real. No, he wasn't wrong. But he sensed a sort of desperation in her love for him, as if she were afraid it would vanish while she watched.

Tucker shifted onto his side again and stared thoughtfully at the moonlit sheen of her hair against the pillowcase. A weekend trip was the only plan he'd been able to devise that might ease the tension and allow him to reassure her.

He studied the faint flicker of her eyelashes as she drifted toward sleep, and his throat grew tight with emotion. Soon she would hear all the words he'd kept inside his heart. Soon the shadow of doubt in her eyes would be gone. Soon . . .

The heat hazed the sky to a shimmery blue. A matched set of cotton-ball clouds hung motionlessly, displaying a supreme indifference to the world at large. The air felt hot enough to bake bread, and the sun beat a relentless warmth into the lazy current of the water.

The fish weren't biting, but Tucker didn't seem to mind. He sat on the grassy bank, his back propped against the trunk of a sturdy oak, one hand holding the fishing rod, the other hand making sketchy circles of pleasure along Kris's bare leg. She lay very still beside him, enjoying the sensations of his nearness, his touch, the shade of the tree, and the cooling breeze that drifted from the water every now and again. She hadn't felt so relaxed in months, years maybe, and it was nice, very nice.

" 'By the shore of Gitche Gumee,/By the shining Big-Sea-Water,/Stood the wigwam of Nokomis,/Daughter of the Moon, Nokomis.' " Kris ended her burst of inspiration with a laugh. "You didn't think I knew any poetry, did you, Tucker?"

"Is this a trick question?"

"Just rhetoric for an idle mind."

"Yours or mine?"

She stared directly overhead at a patch of heaven framed by twisted branches and green leaves. "You're zapping my energy with your questions, Tucker. How can you expect me to remember the rest of the poem if you insist on interrupting my concentration?"

"The idle mind obviously is yours." He took his hand from her knee and shifted his weight. "Mine is busy considering the possibility of a swim." He pointed toward a widening in the creek boundaries. "Gary told me there were places deep enough for swimming."

Kris looked at the inviting pool of dark water. "The correct Maple Ridge terminology is 'swimming hole,' Tucker, but I believe you're beginning to think like a native."

"Poetry always brings out the savage in me." He leaned forward with indolent grace, and the fishing pole dropped uselessly to the ground. "What's the Maple Ridge terminology for 'swimming in the nude'?"

"Now how would *I* know a thing like that?"

"You mean you don't?"

She shook her head and eased herself back to her original recumbent position. "I've never had an occasion to find out."

"Then it's about time you learned." He bent toward her, and she moistened her lips in welcome, but his attention seemed to be focused somewhat lower. Kris watched the lines that fanned with subtle appeal from the corners of his eyes as he unbuttoned her blouse. His hands felt delightfully wicked against her skin.

His steady progress was halted, however, by the shirttail knot she'd tied beneath her breasts. The neckline parted to reveal a creamy vee of gently sloping curves, but his fingers couldn't separate the tangled ends of the blouse. Finally, he met her gaze in defeat. "I'm beginning to understand why you've never learned that particular term, Kristina. It would be easier to toss you in the creek fully clothed."

She smiled and easily worked the knot free. "But you wouldn't do that, would you, Tucker?"

"Just try quoting another line from 'Hiawatha.'"

Her hands reached for him, and the blouse fell open to bare her breasts to his gaze. A reckless longing guided her fingers to press into his shoulders and encourage him to come closer. "How would you feel about Shakespeare? I remember a few lines from—"

He stole the rest of her sentence with a kiss, and a sudden magic filtered into the late-afternoon sunlight: the magic of intimacy shared amid a world that stirred quietly with constant wonder;

the magic of heartbeats blending. It was a perfect moment. And Kris could not hold it close enough.

When Tucker lifted his head, she would not let him go, and he couldn't see any future in struggling against such a lovely captor. He shifted and stretched his length beside her, drawing her into the comfortable circle of his arms. Braced on his side, he could indulge the longing to look at her, to touch her at will, to lose his reason in her gentle fragrance.

Her hair was a wispy halo of disorder; her eyes were an uncompromising gray but misted with moisture. He saw a teardrop form and shimmer uncertainly at the corner of her eye. He watched as she tried to dislodge the drop with a blink of her dark lashes. And then, with tender reverence, he bent to catch the mysterious tear on his lips and prevent its fall.

"Kristina." He breathed her name and tasted the salty trace of her emotion on his tongue.

Her palm came to rest against his cheek; her fingertips brushed a feathery pattern at his temple. At another time or another place he might have questioned the reason for her solitary tear. But somehow Tucker didn't feel it needed explanation. The place, the moment filled his heart with understanding, and he knew why beauty was always in search of a poet. Language was inadequate at times. Words were meaningless in describing a moment that brimmed the edges of forever, yet Tucker yearned to try.

"I love you, Kris," he whispered. "I . . . love you."

For a seemingly endless second he thought she was going to cry, but then, slowly, like the first sweet notes of a ballad, she smiled. It was a smile that made him ache inside, and he thought that if he never drew another breath, he would be content.

Her lips parted in the instant before she claimed his vow. Delicate hands cupped his neck to press him into the fullness of her kiss, and he burned with the sudden fiery intensity of his passion for her.

Kristina gave in to the kaleidoscoping sensations swirling through her and pushed up the hem of his shirt so she could feel him against her bare breasts. Her body clung to his, sculpting thigh to thigh and angles to curves, fitting silken skin to smooth, hard flesh. A sigh of deep contentment wound from her throat as he covered her breast with flicks of his warm, moist tongue.

The weight of her clothing seemed suddenly unbearable, and she struggled to rid herself of its cloying burden. She pushed at the waist of her shorts but tried to maintain a close contact with Tucker's every touch. When he stopped to help her, she knew a pleasurable relief and bribed her impatience with the promise of helping him undress in return.

A cooling breeze caressed her as she raised her hips to allow her clothing to be stripped away. Wanton thoughts drew her restless fingers to the fastening of Tucker's jeans, and soon she was trailing her hand over his legs.

Finally, free of any covering save the streaks of

filtered sunlight, they moved again to the bed of grass and the haven of loving arms. Passion built and ebbed, bringing him to her again and again until the tide of sensual delight crested, leaving her trembling and weak but newly strong.

"I love you, Tucker." She voiced the words that she had waited a lifetime to say and could no longer restrain. With the husky endearment he murmured against her ear, she held him tightly, her heart throbbing with a thousand wistful dreams. Kristina wanted to cry with the sweetness of her emotion. It was as if he had filled her life with beauty, as if she had negotiated the terms of her surrender and at last made peace with the past.

Whatever might come to her in the future, she would not regret the hours spent with him. She loved him. Enough to tell him the truth. Enough to bear the sadness of a pain she'd held within her for too long and now must share with him. But in the midst of that knowledge was the peace of knowing that because he had loved her, she could face her greatest fear . . . and survive.

She lay for an eternal moment, savoring the sounds of his breathing, the rise and fall of his chest beneath her hand, knowing that time had caught up to her fantasy and that soon she would hold only a memory. She was still, waiting for him to break the silence.

"Kristina," he said in a voice filled with emotion, "will you marry me?"

CHAPTER NINE

The shade of the oak tree seemed suddenly the most beautiful spot in the world. Kris thought everything around her took on a new clarity, a new dimension as she savored Tucker's words. *Will you marry me?* Surely this was the memory she would treasure most through all the years to come. From now on summer would remind her of this day, this hour, of being loved by the man she loved. But then wouldn't everything from now on remind her of him?

Sighing, Kris moved away from the contentment of his embrace and sat up. "No."

There was a second of suspended silence before she heard his soft "What?"

"No, Tucker." How could it sound so effortless when her throat was so dry?

He was reaching for her; she felt his touch on her shoulder and quickly shifted away. She couldn't think when he was so near. Standing abruptly, she began to retrieve her scattered clothes, feeling his gaze on her every movement.

"Kristina?"

Her courage almost deserted her when she

heard his achingly confused whisper. She began to pull on her clothes, trying not to look at him, but painfully aware that he was watching her and that he didn't understand. "You don't mean that," he said in a voice edged with humor but trimmed with fear.

She glanced at him, saw the cautious blue of his eyes, and quickly looked away. "I'm . . . sorry." She had to say more, she had to tell him, yet the beginning words wouldn't come. The simple act of buttoning her blouse seemed to demand her complete attention.

Tucker got to his feet and bent to pick up his jeans from the ground, but he continued to stare at Kris as if he thought his gaze alone could fathom the deepest mystery of her emotions. Silently watching her, he dressed, and she trembled with the conflict churning within her. Her hands combed through the sunlit disorder of her hair, rested for a moment at the waistband of her shorts, then slipped inside the front pockets.

"Now, let's talk." His voice was crisp with determination; his stance encouraged no argument. "I asked you to marry me, Kris."

"And I said no."

"Why?"

"Tucker, I—" She swallowed and forced the words to come. "There are things you don't know about me. Things I don't want to tell you."

"Then don't. I love you. There isn't anything you could say that will change that."

How easily he said it. How she wished it could be true. "Tucker, please. I should never have let our relationship progress this far. It was selfish, and I'm—" Her voice trembled, and she paused to steady it. "I'm sorry. I just couldn't seem to help loving you. These past few weeks have been special. . . ." Again her faltering tone betrayed her, and she closed her eyes. Then, with a carefully drawn breath that filled her lungs and braced her courage, she met his eyes. "I love you, Tucker, but I won't marry you."

"I don't know what in hell is going through your mind right now, Kristina, but if you expect me just to walk away from here . . ." This time the tremor was in his voice, but it didn't match the stormy quality of his expression. "Is that what you expect?"

"I . . . think that would be best." She sensed the quick flash of his temper, knew it was a mixture of fear and anger, regretted the fact that it was only the beginning of the disillusionment she had yet to inflict. "It would be easier if we said good-bye now."

"Easier? Than what?" A muscle in his jaw clenched and unclenched, and he rubbed it irritably. "How can you even suggest that our relationship can simply end? Do you honestly think I can just walk out of your life as if nothing happened?"

"Not without an explanation." More than anything in the world she longed to touch him, to ease the apprehension in his eyes with her reassurances. But she had already waited too long. The moment couldn't be postponed anymore, and a sick feeling of acceptance rolled in her stomach.

"Tucker, I love you. I haven't lied to you about that."

He was suddenly still. The water lapped an imaginary echo. *Lied. Lied.* The ugly word seemed to surround her, but she managed to hold her chin steady as she called on an inner reserve of strength. "I have lied to you, though, because I didn't tell you the truth in the beginning. Silence is sometimes as deceptive as an outright lie, you know. I—" Oh, God! Where could she start?

"The first time I met you, Tucker, I thought it was my privilege to paint the truth any color I chose. I didn't see any harm in doing whatever it took to get what I wanted. Eleven years ago I wanted you, so I lied. I told you I was twenty-one, a college sophomore, independent, and in charge of my life." A soft, ironic sigh softened the tense knot in her throat. "I was seventeen, Tucker. A senior in high school, spoiled, reckless, and irresponsible."

She saw the subtle signs of his disbelief, the first faint traces of realization in his expression, and her heart ached. "I didn't intend to change, didn't really have any reason to want to until I met you. My only purpose in coming to the university that weekend was to lose my virginity and thereafter to be able to say I'd *experienced* sex with a college man. I didn't think too much about what I'd have to do to *be* experienced, but it seemed perfectly logical to me at the time." She took her hand from her pocket and restlessly massaged her shoulder. "I planned that weekend right down to the last

156

detail of alibi, but you changed my plans . . . and never even knew that you had."

A shaky laugh eased from her throat. "You believed me. I don't know how, because I was so young, so naïve, but no matter what I said, you accepted it and treated me as if I were the special person I said I was. And because of you, I *felt* older and more mature and special. I loved you then, Tucker, and for that one weekend I valued myself. Do you know that you were the first person ever to *listen* to me? Do you even remember how much we talked in those two days?"

"I remember," he said softly, very softly.

"I was nervous at first when we left the football stadium and went to the after-the-game party. You've probably forgotten. Or maybe I just hid it well. I don't know. But when we got to your apartment, I stopped being nervous and started falling in love." She looked up at the tree branches interlocked overhead, but her memory stayed locked in the past. "It's very easy to fall in love when you're seventeen, and I thought I'd found the key to happiness in your arms. You told me how you felt about the future; you told me there wasn't room in your life for a lasting relationship. But when you're seventeen, it's also very easy to hear only the things you want to hear."

Tucker moved, and Kristina tensed, her gaze swinging to warn him away, to maintain the distance that was vital to her outward calm. He narrowed the margin by only a little and leaned his shoulder against the tree trunk. Then he waited.

Watching her with gentle concern, he simply waited.

"It was a wonderful weekend, Tucker," she began, only to pause with the bittersweet taste of the words on her tongue. "It was the turning point in my life, and I don't regret it. I do regret being so stupidly careless with my youth." She glanced at the grassy creek bank, then forced her eyes back to his. "I was pregnant when I left you that Sunday. Of course, I didn't know. I didn't even think it was possible. I'd borrowed a few birth control pills from a friend, and I thought I was protected, but . . ."

The explanation trailed into a vibrating silence. He was pale, unnaturally still, and she could almost feel the shock that rippled through him. Her hand arched in a nervous gesture, and her mind scurried to find something, *anything* to say. "I thought I had everything planned. I was just so young, very, very young. But that's no excuse—"

Tears stung her eyes, and she pivoted, crossing her arms at her waist as if she could shield herself from his reaction. When his hands cupped her shoulders and pulled her back to lean against him, Kris released her rigid control and accepted his tenderness. His breath stirred warmly at her temple as his arms came around her, and she could feel the rapid beat of his heart.

"Why didn't you tell me as soon as you knew?"

"I wrote to you, Tucker, before I found out about the pregnancy. The first letter was full of my fantasies about our future, and you rejected it within a week. The second letter—"

158

"I sent back unopened." His voice shook with the memory. "My God, Kris, I had no idea. I thought I was saving us both a lot of heartache and . . . What happened? Why didn't you contact me after that? You knew where to find me. You could have reached me somehow. If I'd known . . ."

Kristina sighed and moved away from the comfort of his arms. "I didn't want you to know. After I got the letter back, I knew I had to face the consequences. And I had to face them on my own. For the first time in my life, I accepted responsibility. That was a big step for me, and it wasn't easy, but I did it. Not wisely, I admit, but at the time it seemed the right thing to do. I wasn't mature enough to realize that you had some rights in the situation, too."

She saw the confusion, the questions in his eyes and wished the answers could be different. "No one knows who fathered my child, Tucker. No one. My father would have destroyed you. He's a wealthy man, and he could have ended your career plans with a couple of phone calls. I was old enough to understand that, and I also understood how you felt about becoming a doctor. I'm afraid I had no understanding at all about how you might feel about becoming a parent."

"A parent," he repeated slowly as if he'd only just realized the truth. He turned then, walked to the edge of the water, and stood there. In the long moments that followed, Kris gathered strength to carry the confession through to conclusion. When he came back to her side and reached for her hand, she was prepared.

159

"The baby?" he asked huskily.

"A girl. A very beautiful girl, Tucker, with eyes like yours."

He squeezed her fingers until they ached with the grip. "What went wrong? How did she—why didn't she live?"

In a split second of perception Kris realized his mistake . . . and her own. "She did, Tucker. You have a daughter."

"But . . ." He couldn't seem to complete the thought, and Kristina couldn't seem to do it for him. She could only watch the dawning of comprehension and empathize with his beginning pain. "Dear God, you surely didn't—" His voice broke. "What did you do, Kristina?"

There was no mistaking the accusation in his tone, no way to misinterpret the censure in his eyes. "I gave her up for adoption."

Tucker released her hand quickly and established a small but significant distance between them. "You *gave* my child away, and you never even tried to tell me?"

"It wasn't a matter of *giving* her away, Tucker. There's a little more to it than that, you know."

"No, I don't know. You denied me that and about a thousand other things. Damn!" He took a long stride away from her, then stopped and stared at the ground where only a short time before, he'd made love to her. "How could you do it, Kris? How in heaven's name could you do such an irresponsible thing?"

"It was the only choice I had," she answered, becoming angry in her defensiveness. "And it was

160

the most *responsible* thing I've ever done. And the most difficult. I know this is a terrible shock, Tucker, and for that I'm sorry, but don't start tossing out indictments without knowing the circumstances."

"Oh, I think I can piece those together without too much difficulty. You were under age, and your parents insisted you do the right thing and—"

"My parents insisted I have an abortion! That was their solution. But I didn't do what they wanted, Tucker. I wanted to have your baby. You can't possibly have any idea how badly I wanted that. During the months of the pregnancy I fantasized about someday meeting you again and presenting you with a beautiful, happy, well-adjusted child, so you could see what a great job I'd done as a mother."

"Instead, you've presented me with dozens of uncertainties. God, Kris! She could be unhappy or ill. She might have medical problems or—what if she needed something? We would never even know. Didn't you think about that? Didn't you think about—"

"There isn't one single catastrophe that I haven't imagined, Tucker! There isn't even one tiny possibility that I haven't considered and wondered and worried about during the past ten years. I've thought of them all. And I've thought of all the good things, too. Every small detail of her growing up that I can't share with her. The color of her hair, her height, the pitch of her voice, her smile, her friends, her school activities, her favorite color. Don't stand there and talk to me about doubts. You have no right to—"

"I have no *right* because of you, Kristina. I would have done anything—*anything*—to help you keep the baby if you'd only told me. But you denied me the right to make a decision that affected not only me but my child." His hand formed a slow fist at his side; his eyes were an icy blue. "I don't think I can ever forgive you for that."

The chill slid all the way to her fingertips. "I haven't asked you to, Tucker. I don't *need* your forgiveness. I did what I had to do, and no one, not even you, has the right to judge me for it. You have no idea what that decision has cost me. I made the sacrifices, and I've paid for my mistakes with years of regret. How can you dare talk about *your* rights?"

"Considering that you've just now seen fit to tell me the truth, I think I should be able to say anything I damn well please!"

"Fine, Tucker, you do that. But I don't have to listen. It's easy now for you to point out my mistakes and to feel self-righteous, but try to remember how you felt about life eleven years ago. You didn't want to see me again after that one weekend; you didn't have room in your plans for another person, much less two. You returned my last letter without even reading it and kept your conscience clear. There were no changes in your plans; you didn't have to make any sacrifices. The weekend we spent together was just that for you— a weekend. And you barely even remember that!"

162

She was shaking, and she couldn't bear to look at his coldly remote expression. Spinning with the panicky emotion inside her, Kris bent to pick up her shoes. "I'm going home," she stated, and began walking toward the cabin, not knowing whether he'd heard or cared.

After gathering together the few belongings she'd brought, Kris took them to her car and prepared to leave. She and Tucker had driven to Gary's cabin together in her car, but she simply couldn't sit beside him on the trip home. It was too much to ask. She glanced toward the oak tree, but there was no sign of him, and she couldn't wait. The peaceful area had lost its magic, and she craved the security of home. Tucker could find his own way back . . . if he wanted.

And if he didn't, she would accept that. She'd known the risk from the beginning, known his feelings toward her would change. Her hands trembled on the steering wheel as she guided the car along the winding road. He'd been so angry. In all the times she'd imagined telling him the truth, she hadn't thought his first reaction would be anger. And she'd never thought she would feel so defensive.

No one had ever attacked her decision as Tucker had. Her parents had had a more subtle way of condemning it; they'd finally realized she wouldn't submit to their authority, so they'd sent her to Great-aunt Maudie in Maple Ridge. Kristina could still remember the stern indifference in her father's voice when he'd told her that if she came to her senses, she could come home—alone.

The residents of Maple Ridge had opened their homes and their hearts to Kris, but no one—not even Ruth—had offered advice or opinions on what was the right thing to do. When Kris had returned from the hospital in Russellville without the baby, there had been no judgmental attitudes from her neighbors and friends, only the acceptance and support so characteristic of the people in the community.

Kristina had known she didn't want to return to her parents or to the careless life-style of her past. After her great-aunt had died, leaving the house to Kris, there was no reason to think of anywhere else as home. Almost everyone in town knew the circumstances that had brought Kristina there, but past mistakes were off limits, and it was never discussed. And in all the time that Tucker had lived here, no one had mentioned those circumstances to him. Until today, when she had told him.

Pushing the limp weight of her hair off her neck, Kris braked at a stop sign and then eased through the intersection. Maybe she should have kept the subject off limits. Certainly she wished she hadn't told him about the baby. Maybe it would have been best to keep the secret, to marry Tucker and love him and pretend that honesty in a relationship was unimportant. But of course, it was, and she knew she'd done the right thing in telling him.

No, she corrected herself, the right thing would have been to have done whatever was necessary to get in touch with him years ago. She should have gone to him, made him listen. No matter how devastated she had been by his rejection of her letter, she should have found a way to tell him, to let him participate in the decision.

But would it have made any difference? Somehow Kris didn't believe so. It had been easy today for him to state he would have done anything to help her keep the baby, but would he have said it ten years ago? Would he have sacrificed his career ambitions? Certainly not without experiencing a lot of resentment toward her and the child.

Should. Might. If. What good did it do to think in those terms now? How long would she continue to punish herself for things that could not be changed? She had done what she felt had to be done. She had given up her baby, and she had, finally, told Tucker the truth.

It was over.

CHAPTER TEN

The telephone rang several times before Kristina lifted the receiver in listless answer.

"Kris? What are you doing home?" Jena Saradon asked in a soft, lilting soprano. "I thought you were away for the weekend."

"Why did you call if you thought that?" Kris answered with a smile, feeling cheered simply by the happiness in Jena's voice.

"I was going to leave a message on your answering machine. I wanted you to know as soon as you got back Sunday that you'd missed my entire labor and delivery and the arrival of Baby Saradon."

"Jena! A boy? Or a girl? When? And where are you? I haven't been gone that long. How did you—"

Excitement rippled through the phone wires. "I haven't . . . yet. But believe me, I know the signals. The baby will be born sometime tonight or early tomorrow . . . unless, of course—"

"What about Matt? Is he pacing the floor?"

"He doesn't even know. You know how he is, Kris. He'll make me crazy if I tell him too soon.

When it's time to drive to the hospital, I'll tell him to put his shoes on. That should do the trick."

"One of these times, Jena, you're going to wait too long, and then what are you going to do?"

"This *is* my last time. Four children are my limit. And don't you dare say 'Famous last words.'" Jena's tone softened with subdued excitement. "Don't worry. I won't wait too long, especially considering that we have to drive all the way to Russellville. I certainly wish the new hospital were built already. It would ease Matt's worries, I know. Well, I'd better rest while I can. I'll call you later." There was a pause, and then: "Kris? What happened to the wonderful weekend Tucker had planned for you at Gary's cabin?"

"It rained."

"It did? How odd, we didn't have a drop of precipitation this afternoon. There wasn't even a cloud in the sky."

Kris sighed her admission. "It all depends on your point of view, Jena. Listen, tell Matt to call me from the hospital as soon as the baby is born."

"You'll be one of the first to know," Jena promised. "I'd say 'the first,' except that you know the people in this town. I wouldn't be surprised if someone found out before I did." She laughed. "Bye, Kris. Matt will call you later."

"Good luck, Jena." Kristina replaced the receiver and settled back against the sofa cushions. Tracing a fingertip pattern onto the fabric of a throw pillow, she thought about the Saradons and their new baby. How nice it must have been for Jena to be able to share nine months of planning, to know that the father of her child would be near her during the labor and birth.

Kristina remembered only too well how it felt to face that alone. She had been afraid, unsure of the changes happening within her body and to her emotions. There hadn't been anyone to share with. Her great-aunt Maudie had sat in the living room, crocheting inch after inch of yarn into bright rows but saying hardly a word during all those long months of waiting. Even afterward her only comment had been to tell Kris she could stay in Maple Ridge if she wanted. It had been the loneliest time, the very worst time, in Kristina's life.

The back door opened, and she tensed, knowing she had been listening for that sound ever since she'd arrived home earlier in the day. Tucker was back. She heard his footsteps crossing the kitchen floor, coming toward the living room . . . and her. Her fingers curled into the pillow as she waited for him to find her.

She felt his gaze on her and slowly turned to meet it. He looked tired, and she had a fleeting remembrance of the way he'd looked that day in the courtroom—disenchanted and discouraged. Kristina hurt for him, and she wished there were something she could do. But she realized there was no resolution to their situation. It was impossible. She had known that once he knew the truth, his love for her would be locked behind a dozen other emotions; she'd accepted that, yet she found herself waiting for his smile, waiting for him to say everything was all right.

He said nothing. He only stood watching her. When he walked into the room and sank onto a chair opposite the sofa where she was sitting, her fingers dug a little deeper into the throw pillow.

"I'm sorry I left you stranded at the cabin." Kris tried to clear the nervous flutter from her throat. "I should have waited for you."

"I needed the walk," he said crisply. "And once I reached the main highway, it wasn't hard to get a ride into town."

"Well, anyway I am sorry."

"Don't be. Not about that." It was a cool statement that made her instantly more alert, but Tucker seemed calm and unemotional as he faced her. "Tell me why you gave our child to strangers, Kristina."

"I told you that it wasn't a matter of *giving* her—"

"All right, then. Tell me why you *chose* not to keep her and bring her up yourself."

The bitter edge in his voice made a clean slice through her composure, and her stomach knotted with regrets. "Tucker, I made the best—the only —decision I could make under the circumstances. I had to—"

"*What* circumstances?" he interrupted. With his elbows resting on the arms of the chair and his hands clasped at a forbidding angle across his chest, Kris could feel the intangible strength of his animosity. "I think I deserve at least that much explanation, don't you?"

"I'll tell you whatever you want to know, Tucker, but I think *I* deserve the courtesy of patience. There's no need to interrupt me at every turn."

He dismissed her objection with a shrug. "You have my undivided and *silent* attention."

Kris sighed and eased her grip on the pillow. "I told you how my parents felt. They were very angry with me. At the time I thought it was because an illegitimate grandchild would be a major embarrassment to them. Now that I'm older, I believe it was an anger born of fear. They were afraid I was going to ruin my life by saddling myself with a child. Their concern was for me, not for the baby. And when I refused to have the abortion, my father thought he knew exactly how to handle my rebellious nature. He sent me here to Maple Ridge, the end of the world . . . or so he believed. My great-aunt lived in this house, and I was supposed to go quietly out of my mind with boredom and guilt and eventually realize the wisdom of my parents' advice.

"I'll admit it almost worked, Tucker. Great-aunt Maudie didn't have a lot to say, and even when she did, it didn't make much sense. Not to me anyway. Maybe if I hadn't been quite so headstrong, things might have turned out differently. But the harder my family pressed me to end the pregnancy, the more determined I was to keep the baby. By the time I passed the fifth month all communication between us was cut off. My father was a stubborn man." She paused, remembering. "I suppose he still is."

She lifted her gaze to Tucker's, but he was staring at his hands and wouldn't meet her look. "After a couple of weeks of watching Aunt Maudie crochet, I stopped feeling sorry for myself and took the first step toward maturity. I decided I had to have some means of support for myself and my child, so I enrolled in the local high school and got a part-time job at Ruth's gift shop.

"For months I worked harder than I'd ever imagined anyone could work, but I earned my diploma and managed to accumulate a modest savings account. I also caught a cold that wouldn't get better." Tucker was watching her now, but the past spread a dark shadow between them, and Kristina couldn't think of any way to banish it.

"On the doctor's orders I spent the week before the baby was born in the hospital in Russellville. Resting was supposed to build my strength, but I couldn't sleep or eat. All I could do was think. About you. About the baby. About how I was going to take care of her. It was the lowest point in my life. But when I held her in my arms for the first time, I knew there wasn't a sacrifice that was too great to make for her."

Reminiscent tears changed her voice to a whisper. "It wasn't until the day before I was supposed to bring her home to Maple Ridge that I began to question my decision. I'd known, of course, that I'd have to find someone to stay with her while I worked. Aunt Maudie was too old, and her hearing wasn't very good. All of a sudden I realized what it would *mean* to leave my daughter in another person's care. I began to consider what *her* immediate future was going to be like: a constant shuffle between day care and a baby-sitter at

171

night while I attended classes at a junior college in Russellville. I knew I had to have more education in order to provide even a small measure of security.

"In many ways, Tucker, I was still a child myself. I didn't know who I was. How could I guide such a precious and important life as hers?" Kris smoothed the pillow with her palm and then laid it aside. "Rationalizations, of course, but I was afraid. I'd never had any responsibility at all, and suddenly I felt the weight of more than I'd ever imagined. There was no one to talk with except Ruth, and I'd hardly known her long enough to ask for advice. She never once mentioned adoption, but I could see for myself how much she loved Melinda and Michael."

Tucker shifted his position and leaned forward, listening and yet seemingly very far away. Kristina released long-suppressed emotions on a sigh. "I was unprepared to be a mother. I wasn't even legally an adult, but I was responsible for creating another life—one conceived by accident. Unplanned. Unwanted. I finally took a long look at what I had to offer and realized that it was beyond my ability at that time—physically, mentally, and emotionally—to provide anything more than unlimited love."

She met his intense regard squarely. "That wasn't enough for her, Tucker. If I'd kept her, as I badly wanted to do, the sacrifices wouldn't have been strictly mine. She would have sacrificed the right to be welcomed into a family that had planned and hoped and dreamed for her. She would have paid part of the price for my mistake. The hardest thing I've ever done was to sign those papers, and there hasn't been a day since that I haven't wondered if I did the right thing."

With a ragged breath Tucker dropped his head into his hands and began to rub his temples in slow massage. "Would you do it again?"

The words were rough and uneven, and it took a full minute before Kristina felt the cutting edge of their pain. God! Did he have any idea what he was asking? "Don't, Tucker. I did what I felt I had to do . . . for her. Please don't ask me to make a judgment now. It can't be changed. No matter what."

His gaze snapped to her impatiently. "No more excuses, Kris. I want to know if you'd make the same decision again."

She stood, angry because he was angry, hurting because she knew too well how much he hurt. "Yes, Tucker. Given the same circumstances, yes. Yes, I would." Turning to leave him, she stopped as he took hold of her wrist.

"How could you give her to a stranger, Kristina? How could you do it?" he asked quietly, his anger defeated by the pain that she recognized—the pain that for her had become a soft, ever-present hurt.

"I loved her, Tucker." Her eyes grew misty with emotions. "I . . . loved her." She slipped her hand free and left him then, knowing there was nothing more to be said, nothing more to be done.

Alone in her room she longed for the release of tears, but none would come. Even when she heard the sound of Tucker's car in the night. Even when

173

she realized he had left her home and her life. She comforted herself with logic. She'd been prepared for his leaving, hadn't she? Why should she cry about something she'd known would happen, something she'd accepted long before?

But as the hours crept toward midnight, her acceptance gave way to despair, and she cried for all the things that might have been and now could never be.

The road stretched beyond the headlights like a thread unraveling from a piece of cloth. Endless. Meaningless. Going nowhere because he didn't know where to go. Tucker gripped the steering wheel and pressed down on the accelerator. The Mercedes shot forward in a burst of speed that tightened his hold on the wheel.

What was he doing? he wondered. Why was he risking life and limb in a mindless attempt not to think . . . or feel? It was pointless. He couldn't escape the memory of her voice, the look in her eyes, the knowledge of what she had done. "Oh, Kristina," he moaned softly. "Why did you have to tell me?"

Slowly the car lost speed as Tucker realized the significance of his words. *Why did you have to tell me?* Not "Why didn't you tell me before?" or "Why did you do it?" Not any of the questions he had asked her but a deep-seated wish to turn back the clock, to return to yesterday, when he hadn't known the truth. That was impossible, though. Everything was impossible, except following the highway to some unknown destination. He didn't care where he went as long as it was away from Kristina. Yet the only place he wanted to be was with her.

Flexing the stiffness from his fingers, Tucker stared at his hands. Surgeon's hands, skilled and competent, able to repair and mend a body, but totally inept when it came to matters of the heart. This must be the year for disillusionments, he thought wryly. First the malpractice suit and now Kristina's betrayal. Odd that he felt more threatened by the latter. Six months before, his career had been the focal point of his existence. How quickly that focus had changed to Kris. How easily her town, her friends, her life-style had become his.

Now he felt homeless, a man without a country or a purpose. A surgeon stripped of his confidence, a father robbed of his child. But that wasn't entirely true, he reasoned. His confidence in his professional ability had been slowly returning ever since he'd arrived in Maple Ridge. The lawsuit had been an unpleasant incident, but he had gained a new and valuable perspective on life. The knowledge that he was a father was a tremendous shock, but was it really the betrayal of trust that he'd at first believed?

Tucker guided the car to the shoulder of the road and stopped to consider the possibility. He had analyzed every word Kristina had said, and he had tried to comprehend her reasoning, but perhaps it was time for him to analyze his emotions and motivations. Had he been robbed of his child?

175

Or had he simply been relieved of the obligation to make the decision that Kris had made?

She had tried to contact him, but he'd returned the letter unopened. Why hadn't he read that letter? Had he unconsciously been protecting himself from any possible responsibility? He had been idealistic and ambitious at that point in his life. God! Hadn't he told Kristina there was no room in his schedule for her? And there certainly hadn't been room for any mistakes.

But he had made mistakes. Innocent ones, but mistakes just the same. She shouldn't have lied to him, but then he'd been old enough to recognize her inexperience, and still he'd ignored the clues as if they hadn't existed. She had been vulnerable, and he had thoughtlessly taken advantage. Then he had sent her on her way without so much as a "see you later." And when she'd written to tell him of the consequences of their special weekend, he hadn't bothered to read her letter.

Tucker brushed a weary hand through his hair and stared at the twin beams of the headlights reaching futilely into the darkness. He couldn't understand why Kristina hadn't tried again to contact him, but he couldn't entirely blame her either. How could he honestly say what his reaction would have been if he'd known about the baby? He had been a different person then, full of his own plans and importance. What right did he have to judge Kris for making a decision she felt was best?

He loved her. No matter how he felt about anything else, he knew that hadn't changed. He couldn't deny, though, that the knowledge of his paternity made a difference in his relationship with Kristina, bonding them in one way, separating them in another. But how could he justify his impulsive departure from her life? He needed to talk to her, wanted to share his uncertain thoughts and feelings with her. After all, when it came down to the bottom line, who else could possibly understand?

In sudden decision he started the car and made a U-turn onto the highway. The Mercedes skimmed the miles as Tucker watched for familiar road signs. He hadn't realized he'd driven so far, but it seemed to take hours to reach the outskirts of town. It was after midnight, and Maple Ridge was quiet as he drove through the streets, past the unfinished construction that would soon be a hospital, past the municipal building and the *Gazette* office, past Ruth's shop and the grocery. For a few minutes Tucker savored the pleasant feeling of being a part of this community and knew that he didn't want to leave.

Kristina's house was dark except for the pale light that illuminated the back porch steps. He turned onto the graveled driveway and saw Kris standing beside the opened door of her car. In the glare of his headlights she lifted a hand to shade her eyes, and he smiled at the enchanting picture she made. Her hair was a disheveled halo of silvery gold. She was dressed in faded blue jeans and one of his shirts. He hadn't realized he'd left the shirt behind, but it pleased him somehow that she was wearing it now.

As he stopped the car directly behind hers, Kris ran to the passenger side of the Mercedes and pulled open the door. "Tucker," she said in a breathy rush, "I'm on my way to the Saradons'. Jena's in labor, and Matt can't get his truck to start."

"Get in. I'll go with you." He waited for Kris to slide onto the seat beside him before he reversed and backed from the driveway. Despite the tension of the afternoon and evening, Tucker felt a sudden sweet delight in being close to her again. "If this is a code three," he said lightly, "you can be the siren and I'll blink the lights."

Her gaze came to his in momentary surprise. "Just concentrate on driving as fast as you safely can. When Jena called, she said there wasn't any great hurry, but I could hear Matt in the background yelling something about the National Guard. He goes a little crazy at times like this."

"I suppose most men do at times like this."

A tiny smile touched Kristina's lips and Tucker's heart. "I suppose. At least Jena is calm. She said she really wouldn't mind having the baby at home, but I'm not sure Matt would survive. Having you there might help."

"Why?"

"You're a doctor, Tucker."

"A surgeon, Kris. I haven't delivered a baby since my pre-med days, and I really would prefer to keep it that way."

"But in an emergency?"

"I'll drive faster. Whatever the record time is in getting from here to the nearest hospital, I'll break

178

it." He slowed the car to make a left turn. "We'll just keep our fingers crossed that Jena is right and that the new Saradon heir isn't in a great hurry to be born."

Kristina said nothing, and when Tucker glanced at her inquiringly, he sensed that her thoughts were far away. She was pleating a fold in the material of his shirt, but her eyes were focused on something beyond the boundaries of the night. A question formed in his mind and dropped, unbidden, into the quiet. "Was our baby in a hurry to be born, Kris?"

The subsequent hesitation lasted a seemingly endless second. "No. I guess she knew I needed all the growing-up time possible before she made her appearance in the world. Even when the labor started, she wasn't in a hurry."

Tucker searched for words to express something, he wasn't sure what. But there was nothing to say. Not now.

"Amber," Kris said in a throaty whisper. "I don't know what her name is, but I think of her as Amber. In a way you chose that name, Tucker. After the first time we made love in front of the fireplace, you told me you'd remember me always in amber. It seemed fitting to give our daughter a name that was a symbol of the happiness we shared for one weekend."

The Saradon mailbox gleamed a silvery welcome, and Tucker felt both relief and regret that there wasn't time to reply. *Amber*, he thought. His daughter . . . and Kris's.

"What took you so long?" Matt jerked open

179

Tucker's door even before the car came to a stop in the driveway. "My wife is having a baby, you know. Jena, will you come on?" He motioned toward Jena, who was sitting on the porch steps complacently watching the proceedings as if she had a front-row ticket for the Saturday night fights.

With a worried sigh Matt retraced his steps, helped Jena to her feet, picked up her small suitcase, and led her to the Mercedes. Tucker exchanged a brief sharing glance with Kristina, and then both expectant mother and father were inside the car, and it was time to go.

The trip to Russellville was made in record time and was marked by an uneventful conversation between Kris and Jena. Tucker said little, and Matt maintained an obviously painful silence that ended abruptly at the entrance to the hospital. Matt ordered everyone inside as if he were a general in charge of army maneuvers, and then, the moment Jena was whisked away by a smiling nurse, he promptly collapsed and had to be led to the nearby waiting room.

As one hour slipped into two, Tucker watched Matt's nervous attempts to appear calm, but his thoughts were on Kristina. She sat opposite him, her head bent as she leafed through the pages of a magazine, her hair drifting about her shoulders in a loose caress. Once, Tucker thought, she had been on the other side of these hospital walls. But there had been no one waiting and worrying for her, not even her great-aunt Maudie, who had been too frail to make the trip. No one had cared the way the three of them did for Jena.

Kristina had been alone. Suddenly the enormity of that fact wove through him, leaving his heart to throb a slow, heavy rhythm of comprehension. She had been only seventeen, just out of high school, physically and emotionally drained, and she had borne his child alone. He had a strange impulse to apologize to her, but he kept silent and waited for something to ease the tension.

When at last the phone in the waiting room rang and Matt hurried to meet his newborn son, Tucker stood and rubbed the back of his neck. "I didn't know the worst part of having a baby would be the waiting. Do you suppose they'll name him after me?"

Kris looked up and tried to smile. "I doubt it. You really didn't do anything particularly heroic."

Tender concern welled inside him at the tired expression in her eyes. "Would you consider the simple act of taking you home as something akin to heroism?"

"You could get a medal if you break the all-time return trip record. Probably we should wait for Matt, though. He'll want to get back to Maple Ridge and tell the other Saradon siblings about their new brother." She paused, and this time the smile seemed almost normal. "I might warn you that if you expect a quiet ride, you're bound for disappointment. Matt will more than make up for what he didn't say on the way here."

"I can handle a proud father's excitement if you can."

They waited in agreeable quiet for several minutes. "Kristina," Tucker said softly, "I wish I had been here with you when our—when Amber was born."

A betraying quiver tugged at the corners of her lips. "So do I."

He wanted to say more, to comfort her, but instead, he sank onto the chair again, clasped his hands, and waited for Matt's return. It was difficult to wait, but Tucker decided it was fitting for him to be here, in this hospital with Kris.

Too late but very fitting.

CHAPTER ELEVEN

The trip home from the hospital was all Kris had predicted . . . and more. Matt broke the all-time record for nonstop conversation on a single topic. He talked with all the excitement and enthusiasm of a new father who realizes that no one is actually listening but who doesn't really care. Kris couldn't restrain her sigh of relief when at last Matt stepped out of the car at his house and expressed— not for the first time—his eternal gratitude and the promise of a steak dinner reward as soon as Tena and the baby were home.

Tucker didn't linger long enough to encourage any more discussion on the topic of the Saradon family. He said a hasty good-bye and abruptly drove away. As the last shadow of night closed around the Mercedes, a cautious awareness crept into the sudden quiet. Kris accepted the silence, knowing that it was composed of Tucker's uncertainties as well as her own. It seemed impossible that less than twenty-four hours had passed since they'd made love in the shade of the oak tree. Her body trembled with the memory and the thought that she might never feel his touch again.

What was he thinking? she wondered. Were his thoughts on her, or were they focused on that distant summer? She turned the hem of her shirt-tail into a tight roll and then released it. Had Tucker noticed that she was wearing his shirt? Silly thought. It was so obviously *his*. How could he help noticing? She felt a little embarrassed at being caught in such a peculiarly feminine weakness. But when he'd left her, putting on the shirt he'd left behind had been the only comfort she could find.

And now he was back. What did it mean? Kris couldn't begin to answer all the questions in her mind. She could only sit next to him and wish that the taut silence would end. She was very good at wishing. There were times when it seemed as if she'd spent most of her life wishing for something she couldn't have.

Tucker glanced at her, and Kristina offered a tentative smile, but it wasn't returned, and the tension became a heavy ache in her lungs. She couldn't halt the weary sigh that escaped her when Tucker drove up her driveway and stopped the Mercedes beside her house. Streaks of morning lightened the eastern sky and faded the glare of the porch light to a dim fluorescence.

The air was very still as Kristina stepped from the car and paused to listen to the quiet sounds of a new Sunday morning. She closed the door and waited, not knowing whether to hope Tucker would leave again without explanation or to wish that he would stay. When she heard his door open

184

and close, she released the breath she hadn't realized she was holding.

As he walked to her side, Kris tried to think of a casual sentence to break the silence and knew it was wasted effort. She turned to him with the half-formed idea that her heart would know what to say. But the instant her eyes met his, her throat tightened with emotion, and when his lips tipped upward in a tender curve, she longed to walk straight into his arms.

"I didn't expect to see you again, Tucker," she whispered hoarsely. "Ever."

He thrust his hands into the pockets of the jacket he wore and looked past her shoulder before letting his gaze slowly return. "When I left, I didn't expect to come back. I'm not sure what I'm doing here now, but as I was driving away from Maple Ridge, all I could think about was what I had left behind, and I knew I had to talk to you."

A momentary frown creased his forehead. "I really like this town, Kris, and the people. Helping Jena and Matt tonight made me realize how important it is to be involved with other people. For such a long time I've been totally involved with my career, letting every other area in my life slide into second place . . . until you came along. How did you happen to walk into that courtroom on the very day I needed you, Kris? At any other time I might have been too busy with professional demands to recognize the bond that existed between us even on that first day. I could so easily have missed falling in love with you again."

"How did you happen to be at the University of

185

Missouri football game on the very day I was looking for someone to love?" She lifted her shoulders in a transient shrug. "I can't explain it, Tucker. There just are so many things I simply have no answer for. I think I went to the courtroom to see you because I was searching for a link to my daughter. My love for her is woven into my love for you. But then everything I care about is somehow woven into the way I feel about you."

His gaze turned to the sunrise, and Kristina felt his doubts, his uncertainties as if they were her own. "I never wanted to hurt you, Tucker. Please believe that."

"Have you told me everything, Kristina?" he asked after a while. "Is there anything else about the past that you feel I should be told?"

"No, you know the worst."

"And the best." His gaze came back to hers. "I love you. Will you marry me?"

Her breath caught and then winged to her lips in soft, sweet surprise. "Tucker, I—yes. Yes, if you're sure . . ."

With a gentle, fleeting smile he brought her into his arms and cradled his palm on her cheek. "I've never been more sure of anything, Kristina. You are my future. Maple Ridge is home to me now. I want to belong here, to be a part of this community, to have a voice in shaping its growth. I want to share my life with you. I would like to have a family—children who are planned and anticipated and welcomed."

His lips caressed the corners of her mouth, his hand slipped into the silky texture of her hair, and

Kris thought she would drown in the wonder of his touch. "I love you," she murmured, "but I never dared hope. . . . I believed you'd hate me when you knew—"

"I learned a lot tonight, Kris." He raised his head to look solemnly into her eyes. "I thought at first that I could never forgive you for giving our child to strangers, but I realized while we were waiting at the hospital that it wasn't a question of forgiveness. For a few minutes tonight I saw how it must have been for you. Jena had Matt's love and support; she had friends and family waiting to share her excitement.

"You were alone, Kris, separated from everything and everyone you cared about. I can only imagine how terrible that must have been for you, how very difficult it must have been to bear a child under those circumstances. It seems so pointless to say I wish I might have shared that time with you, but I do wish . . ."

His voice faltered into longings that Kristina understood only too well. "I know, Tucker. I've lived with those same wishes for a lot of years. After a while it stops hurting quite so much."

"I know you did what you felt was best for our child, Kris, even though I'm just beginning to realize what that decision meant to you. You sacrificed your peace of mind for the belief that an adoptive family could give her a loving welcome and the secure future that you couldn't provide. I can't honestly say I think you made the right decision, but then I can't honestly say it was the wrong one either. I guess the doubts and the regrets will linger for the rest of our lives, Kris."

"Maybe someday she'll find us, Tucker. That isn't impossible, you know." Kris traced a comforting finger along his eyebrow and down his cheek to his mouth.

He kissed the tip of her finger with warm promise. "We can wish for that. And in the meantime, we're going to be happy. That isn't impossible either, you know."

The smile came straight from her heart, and Tucker shared it for an endlessly sweet moment before he met her lips in an oh-so-tender kiss. The doubts, the uncertainties, and the regrets might always be a part of their relationship, she realized, but only a part. The secrets and the shadows of her love for him were gone forever. She could face anything as long as Tucker was there to share it with her.

Sunrise christened the morning with bright color as Kris surrendered the past and the future, fantasy and reality, into her lover's capable hands. And in exchange she captured the present—the incredible miracle of now—for herself and for Tucker.

She heard the muffled ringing of the telephone inside the house and felt a pleasurable sense of homecoming. "The Maple Ridge grapevine is right on schedule," she said happily. "That will be Ruth calling to tell us about the addition to the Saradon household."

"Then she'll be the first one to be invited to our wedding. Do you think she'll be surprised?"

188

"If I know Ruth . . . and I do . . . she'll be the first one to congratulate herself on doing a great job of matchmaking. But to us she'll say that it's about time we had the good sense to realize what the rest of the town has known for weeks."

Tucker pulled Kristina closer. "Maybe we should let Ruth and the rest of the town speculate a little longer. What do you think?"

"I think you have better sense than even I gave you credit for."

He kissed her again, lingering as their love warmed the caress to desire. "I love you, Kristina DuMont. Will you spend this Sunday with me?"

"This Sunday . . . and all the other days of my life."

As they walked hand in hand up the porch steps and into the house, the telephone continued to ring. Without a second's compunction Kristina lifted the receiver and dropped it onto the sofa cushions, leaving it—and the residents of Maple Ridge—to dangle, while she began the day . . . and the rest of her life . . . with Tucker.

Candlelight
Ecstasy Romances™

$1.95 each

At your local bookstore or use this handy coupon for ordering:

DELL READERS SERVICE-Dept. B605B
P.O. BOX 1000, PINE BROOK, N.J. 07058

Please send me the above title(s) I am enclosing $_____ (please add 75¢ per copy to cover postage and handling.) Send check or money order—no cash or CODs. Please allow 3-4 weeks for shipment.

Ms./Mrs./Mr._____

Address_____

City/State_____ Zip _____